Jess circled around the car, where a steady drip fell from an open tube. Someone had cut her brake line.

She pushed herself to her feet, a chill sweeping over her.

Accidents can happen.

"Car trouble?"

The deep male voice behind her sent panic shooting through her. The note fluttered to the pavement as she spun and fell back into a fighting stance. Shane stood only four feet in front of her and quickly increased the distance, hands raised.

"Remind me never to sneak up on you."

Relief cascaded over her, and she pressed a hand to her heart. "You startled me."

He grinned. "I noticed. Is something wrong?"

She picked up the sheet of paper. "I found this taped to the driver window. Someone cut the brake line."

His green eyes scanned the page she held, and his strong jaw tightened. The quiet fury that passed over his features sent a funny little flutter through her stomach.

That wasn't just neighborly concern she saw there.

Books by Carol J. Post

Love Inspired Suspense

Midnight Shadows
Motive for Murder

CAROL J. POST

From medical secretary to court reporter to property manager to owner of a special events decorating company, Carol's résumé reads like someone who doesn't know what she wants to be when she grows up. But one thing that has remained constant through the years is her love for writing. She started as a child, writing poetry for family and friends, then graduated to articles, which actually made it into some religious and children's publications. Several years ago (more than she's willing to admit), she penned her first novel. In 2010, she decided to get serious about writing fiction for publication and joined Romance Writers of America, Tampa Area Romance Authors and Faith, Hope & Love, RWA's online inspirational chapter. She has placed in numerous writing contests, including RWA's 2012 Golden Heart®.

Carol lives in sunshiny central Florida with her husband (who is her own real-life hero) and writes her stories under the shade of the oaks in her yard. She holds a bachelor's degree in business and professional leadership, which doesn't contribute much to writing fiction but helps a whole lot in the business end of things. Besides writing, she works alongside her music minister husband singing and playing the piano. She also enjoys sailing, hiking, camping—almost anything outdoors. Her two grown daughters and grandson live too far away for her liking, so she now pours all that nurturing into taking care of three fat and sassy cats and one highly spoiled dog.

MOTIVE FOR MURDER

CAROL J. POST

HARLEQUIN® LOVE INSPIRED® SUSPENSE

Recycling programs
for this product may
not exist in your area.

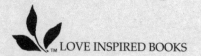

™ LOVE INSPIRED BOOKS

ISBN-13: 978-0-373-67596-8

MOTIVE FOR MURDER

Copyright © 2014 by Carol J. Post

www.Harlequin.com

Printed in U.S.A.

He heals the brokenhearted
and binds up their wounds.
—*Psalms* 147:3

Thank you to my family—Kristi, Andrea, Kim, Jerry, Robbie, Sheri, Keith, Mom Post, Mom Roberts and Jesse—for your unending encouragement and support. And thanks, Mom Roberts, for buying my books for all of your friends!

To my wonderful critique partners, Karen Fleming, Dixie Taylor and Sabrina Jerema. I don't think I could do this without you.

To my amazing editor, Rachel Burkot, and my awesome agent, Nalini Akolekar, thank you. I am thrilled to be working with both of you.

And always, thanks to my wonderful husband, Chris. You are the love of my life.

ONE

The house stood silhouetted against a cloudless sky, the landscape frozen and still under the onslaught of one of Central Florida's infrequent cold fronts.

Just like the last time she had stepped foot on this property.

Jessica Parker drew in a deep breath and threw open the car door, stopping short of dinging the shiny red Lotus sitting next to her Bug. As she stepped into the frigid night air, she pulled her coat more tightly around her, the cold outside mirroring the chill within. Eight long years, and nothing had changed. The same huge oak shadowed most of the front yard. The same potted plant waited by the front door, hiding the key to the house. And as she made her way up the cracked cement drive, she was hit with the same lack of warmth that she had always associated with home.

She squatted to tilt the pot, then heaved a sigh. The key was gone. Priscilla was still messing with her, even from beyond the grave. She straightened and walked back to her car to grab a screwdriver. It had been years since she had picked a lock. But that wasn't a skill easily forgotten—like riding a bike.

The sliding glass door was her best bet. It had been her most frequent middle-of-the-night point of entry after her sister had locked her out. Priscilla's favorite pastime had always been thinking of ways to get her in trouble. Of course, Jessica had given her plenty to work with. But those days were over. She was a law-abiding citizen now.

She rounded the back of the house. Good, no Charley bar. A sliding glass door without it would be no match for a screwdriver in practiced hands. She squatted and slipped the flat tip under one of the doors. A twig snapped a short distance away. Her senses shot to full alert, and she eased to her feet, gripping the tool like a weapon. But all was still. Eerily so.

Of course it was. This was Harmony Grove, not Miami. At two in the morning, all its citizens would be home in bed, fast asleep. Shaking off the last of the uneasiness, she resumed her work on the locked door, then slid it back in its track. She hadn't lost her touch.

Her confident smile faded the instant she stepped into the kitchen and flipped the light switch. Every cabinet door was open. Dishes and utensils filled both sinks and covered the countertops in haphazard stacks. Pots and pans littered the floor, and the overflow occupied the four-person table. Her sister had grown up to be quite the slob. It would take days to get everything clean and back into the cabinets. Especially with no dishwasher.

Irritation surged up inside her, with guilt on its tail. She had tried to set aside her animosity toward her sister, now more than ever. But this was so typical of Priscilla. Acting with total disregard for anyone who might be affected by her selfish decisions.

A closer look, though, shattered her initial assessment. These weren't dirty dishes. In fact, there wasn't a dirty plate, glass or piece of silverware in the bunch. What was Priscilla doing? Why empty all the cabinets?

Jessica pushed a stack of pans away from the edge of the table to clear a spot for her purse, then hung her jacket over the back of a chair. When she reached the end of the counter, she stopped in the open doorway of the living room. Decorative throw pillows littered the floor, and couch cushions rested at haphazard angles, as if Priscilla had been looking for something. She moved farther into the room. A photo frame lay facedown on the end table, and she reached to stand it up. Priscilla stared back at her, sending an unexpected jolt coursing all the way to her toes.

Jessica drew in a steadying breath. She had buried the past and moved forward with her life. And she had done well. Then she got that phone call. And now she was back. It was hard to keep the past buried when she was surrounded by it, memories dogging her at every turn, a blond-haired princess accusing her with those crystal-blue eyes.

She picked up the frame for a closer look. Priscilla had grown up to be quite pretty. She had been a chubby-cheeked thirteen-year-old when Jessica left, with a lingering childishness and an angelic innocence that fooled ninety percent of the people she met. The woman in the photo looked neither childish nor innocent. Though she wore a pleasant half smile, her features held hardness, hinting at a life that had knocked her around and the barriers that had gone up as a result.

What had happened? What could be so bad that she believed she had nothing to live for? Why does anyone take their own life?

She set the frame back on the table and kicked a pillow aside. Two bedrooms waited for her down the hall, likely in the same shape as the other rooms. She stopped at the first open doorway, and dread washed over her. No, this was much worse.

It was her and Priscilla's room, frozen in time—the twin beds and their whitewashed headboards, the chest with five drawers, three of which Prissy had always managed to claim, and the mismatched vanity, which Prissy took over from day one. They had always had to share a room. And Jessica had hated every minute of it.

But the mess made the room almost unrecognizable. Every dresser drawer had been pulled out, clothes scattered from one end of the room to the other. The contents of the closet contributed to the disarray. Cloth-covered hangers, even a pair of crutches, jutted up from the chaos at odd angles. This wasn't Priscilla's doing. Someone had ransacked the house.

She backed into the hall, ready to call the police. But she didn't make it far. As she reached the living room, a muffled squeak sounded in the kitchen. Like the rubber sole of a tennis shoe against the vinyl-tile floor.

Apprehension sifted over her, raising the fine hairs on the back of her neck. She stood frozen, ears cocked for any sign that she wasn't alone, mind ticking through her options. Her phone was in the kitchen with her purse. So was anything she could use as a weapon. If she had to defend herself, it would be through hand-to-hand combat.

A face appeared around the wall separating the kitchen from the living room, then disappeared a nanosecond later. Her heart began to pound and her muscles tensed as adrenaline pumped through her body. Someone was in the house. And not knowing whether he was armed or had brought buddies, she decided that standing her ground and fighting was a last resort.

She bolted toward the front door. Heavy footsteps sounded behind her. She would never get the door open before he reached her. Her best weapon was the element of surprise. At five foot three and a hundred twenty pounds, no one expected her to pack a hard punch.

Or a devastating kick.

She spun to face him, disconcerted at how much ground he had covered in such a short time. She had less than a second to respond. She raised a knee and thrust outward with a boot-clad foot. It contacted with a thud and a whoosh of forcefully exhaled air. The impact sent him flying backward onto his rear. But he didn't stay there. In fact, he didn't really land there, just used the whole experience as a launch into a backward somersault that brought him effortlessly to his feet.

At least he wasn't armed. Not that she could see anyway. She couldn't vouch for what might be hiding under that black leather jacket.

Whatever it was, she wasn't going to give him a chance to reach for it. She charged forward, feet flying. A well-placed kick to the gut doubled him over, but he managed to turn and deflect the majority of the follow-up punch to the face. A steely hand clamped around her wrist, thrusting her forward and flinging her to the floor in front of the entertainment center. He hurled himself toward her, but before he could pin her, she was back on her feet, ready with a kick to the chest.

His body slammed backward into the coffee table with the crack of splintering wood and the crash of shattering glass. One more kick should put him down for the count. But she never got the opportunity. In one smooth motion, his hand swept inside his jacket and emerged with a pistol. It was pointed at her chest.

"Sit. Over there. On the couch."

His voice was husky. She liked to think it was from the blows she had delivered. For several moments she stood unmoving, except for the rapid rise and fall of her chest. Her heart pounded and her mind churned. A low crescent kick would probably send the gun flying. It could also get her killed. Not worth taking a chance.

But she wasn't ready to back down. If he intended to shoot her, he would have done it already. "Who are you?"

He raised himself to a seated position, eyeing her cautiously. "How about if you talk first, considering I *am* the one with the gun." He flashed her a smile that would have appeared amicable without said gun. "Tell me what you're doing sneaking in here in the middle of the night."

She stared down at him, trying to size him up. She had never seen him before. If she had, she would have remembered him. If not the sandy blond hair that fell around his face and neck with careless abandon, then those warm green eyes with their golden flecks. Or his perfect white teeth.

He was exactly the type she would have gone for a few years ago—wild and carefree, with just enough bad boy to keep things exciting. But she had learned her lessons. And she wasn't going there again, well-fitting dress jeans and black leather jacket aside.

"So are you going to answer me?"

His eyes held hers a moment longer. Then she threw back her head and laughed. She had known that the town of Harmony Grove wouldn't roll out the welcome mat for her. But she hadn't expected to be greeted like this, either.

Welcome home.

Shane Dalton eased onto one hip and shook his head. The woman was certifiably nuts. But she had some wicked kicks. He was just going to restrain her until he could find out who she was and what she was doing there. But those boots. They seemed to come out of nowhere. And he was hard-pressed to accomplish what he needed without striking back.

He pressed a finger to his left nostril, trying to stem the trickle of blood that grew worse the longer he was upright. He needed a wet rag. An ice pack wouldn't hurt, either. His head throbbed, with most of the pain concentrated on his nose. If he hadn't turned when he did, she would have broken it. The woman's punches were as deadly as her kicks.

He pushed himself to his feet, determined not to wince. He was so going to pay for this tomorrow. And judging from her satisfied smirk, she knew exactly how much of a beating she had dished out.

"Well?" he prodded.

Except for two brief times when her gaze flicked

to his weapon, her eyes never left his. Now that he was standing, at least as straight as his protesting body would allow, she was forced to look up, even with those killer platform boots.

"This is my house."

He cocked a disbelieving brow. "And do you regularly enter your house at two a.m. via a screwdriver?"

"When I don't have a key."

He took several steps back and, once out of reach of those lethal feet, lowered his weapon and leaned against the wall. He was starting to ache all over. "And I assume the Harmony Grove Police would confirm that?"

She raised her chin a little higher. His implied threat to call the police hadn't rattled her in the slightest. Her eyes held a challenge, delivered with a confidence that bordered on cockiness. Her dark hair was cut in a bob, short and sassy, and a burgundy sweater and black jeans molded themselves to a body that was lithe and athletic. Of course, he had already experienced some of that athleticism firsthand.

"Tell me your name."

"Jess Parker. Like I told you, this is my house. At least, it's my family's house."

"Priscilla's sister."

"Yes, and the Harmony Grove Police *would* confirm that." She lifted one foot to rest on the only piece of the coffee table frame that was still vertical, wedging its point in the arch of her boot. "And who are you?"

"Shane Dalton, your new neighbor."

She gave him the same look he had given her earlier, full of skepticism. "And you regularly follow single women into their homes in the middle of the night and accost them?"

"If they look suspicious enough."

Her gaze narrowed further. "If we're neighbors, where do you live?"

"Right over there." He pointed out the front window to a building that sat kitty-corner.

"That's Yesteryear Antiques."

"I know. There's an apartment over the store. I just moved in today."

"And the Harmony Grove Police would confirm that?"

He restrained the urge to laugh. She was a master at turning the tables. "I don't know about the Harmony Grove Police. But I'm sure the Harrisons would, since they're the ones who collected my rent."

She dropped her foot to the floor and planted both hands on her hips. "That still doesn't explain what you were doing here in the middle of the night. Armed, I might add."

He gave her a half smile. "You're not very trusting, are you?"

"Let's just say I haven't met many people who are deserving of trust. So answer my question."

"I couldn't sleep. I was looking out the window, saw you pull up and start looking for a way into the house. I figured I'd better check you out." It was the truth. Just not the whole truth. "Not knowing your intentions, I decided to grab my gun. Turns out, I needed it."

She lowered her fists from her hips, but gave no indication that she believed him. "Moving into a new neighborhood and accosting its women is a good way to get yourself killed." Her tone was scolding.

"Somehow Harmony Grove doesn't strike me as a dangerous kind of place. Besides, I didn't accost you. If you'll notice, you hardly have a hair out of place, while I'm the one trying to keep from bleeding all over my fancy leather jacket."

One side of her mouth slid upward into a crooked grin, and she brushed past him on her way to the kitchen. "Come on, let's get you cleaned up. Are you bleeding anywhere else?"

"I haven't taken inventory, but I think this is it. The rest is internal."

"I'm sure you'll live." She lifted a towel from a folded stack on the counter and held it under a stream of cold water. "And the table? You didn't get cut?"

"My jacket kept most of the glass out of my back." He removed the item to inspect it. The leather had fared well. Other than a couple of small nicks, it had come through the ordeal unscathed. The glass was probably tempered.

Once he had hung the jacket on the back of one of the kitchen chairs, she pulled the chair out and pushed him onto it.

"Hold still," she commanded, and began wiping the blood from his nose and lip. Her touch was amazingly gentle, considering she had used him as a punching bag only moments earlier.

"Where did you learn to fight like that?"

"Six years of tae kwon do. I'm a second-degree black belt."

"I see." That would have been nice to know ahead of time.

But he hadn't gotten any real intel yet. He had been working an assignment in Lakeland, a plane that went down near the airport carrying seven hundred fifty pounds of pure cocaine. The pilot evidently escaped unharmed. There were no bodies and no reports of anyone seeking medical attention for injuries consistent with a plane crash. Since then, he and his team had spent two months undercover and had come up with zilch.

Then this afternoon he got word that someone had called in an anonymous tip. A young waitress in nearby Harmony Grove had been making large cash deposits into her account for the past two and a half months. And she had supposedly just killed herself. Maybe it was related to the case he was working, maybe it wasn't. But it was the only lead he had had so far. So he had rushed over to Harmony Grove, secured the apartment and settled back to wait until after dark to start his investigation. Except this Jess Parker had thrown a monkey wrench into his plans.

She moved to the counter to retrieve another towel, this time wrapping some ice inside. "Here, hold this against your face."

He grinned up at her, as well as he could with a rapidly swelling lip. "Do you always provide medical treatment to your victims, or is this your form of an apology?"

"Uh-uh. I'm not apologizing for beating you up. You shouldn't have been in my house."

All right. He would give her that. His gaze circled the ransacked room. "So what do you think they were looking for?"

"I don't know." Her answer came without hesitation. She didn't know, or wasn't willing to tell him?

He locked gazes with her. He could usually spot a liar. The eyes and facial expressions gave it away every time. But reading her wasn't going to be easy. Her dark eyes were guarded, her real thoughts hidden behind a facade of toughness. Penetrating it would require getting to know her. The idea intrigued him, beyond its impact on the case.

He slapped aside the thought. His career didn't lend itself to developing romantic relationships.

"Anything your sister might have been involved in that was a little shady? Something she might have had possession of that someone didn't want the authorities to find?"

She shrugged, as nonchalant as if they were discussing a soft drink choice. "I wouldn't have a clue. I haven't talked to her in eight years."

Eight years? That was hard to believe. "Why so long?"

She raised her chin and crossed her arms. "Not that it's any of your business, but my sister and I never got along. Actually, I didn't get along with my parents, either. When I turned eighteen, I took off and never looked back." She flashed him a smile, but there was no humor in it. "I'm guessing the town of Harmony Grove threw a big party."

He nodded slowly. Troubled childhood. That explained some of her hard edge. "Are you going to stay here?"

"Not permanently. But since no one can find my mother and whatever man she's currently with, all of this falls on me. Once I get it resolved, I'm heading back to Miami."

"The reason I ask is I'm not sure how safe you are here. Whoever did this might be back."

"Maybe. But he won't get in. I'm going to screw the stationary slider into place and install a Charley bar to secure the other one."

"Good. Do you think they found what they were looking for?"

"I don't know. As near as I can tell, the whole place has been turned upside down. The only rooms

I haven't checked are the master bedroom and the two baths."

"I see."

His gaze circled the kitchen, then came back to settle on the woman in front of him. This Jess Parker was a little rough around the edges. Was she part of whatever Priscilla had gotten involved with? Or was she just going to get in his way?

Actually, she already had. He needed to search the place. Somewhere in the mess were clues that could help him in his investigation. But searching with her there was going to be almost impossible. Unless he did so right under her nose.

"Would you like some help with this?"

She eyed him with raised brows. "Why would you do that?"

"Just being neighborly."

"You don't have a job to go to or something?"

"No, I just arrived this afternoon, remember?"

She shrugged, but still didn't respond to his question. "So what do you do? Normally, I mean. When you *are* working."

"A little of this, a little of that. So feel free to put me to work."

She studied him for several more moments, then gave a brief dip of her head. "All right. Tomorrow. Now I'm going to get some sleep."

He rose from the chair and stepped toward the open sliding glass door. "Lock this behind me." He flashed her a teasing smile, accompanied by a wink. "You never know what kind of riffraff might come through."

"Yeah, I learned that tonight."

As she clicked the lock into place, he rubbed his bruised ribs. Whatever came through that door, she could probably handle it.

TWO

Jessica let herself into the house, juggling a McDonald's coffee, an egg and sausage biscuit and the morning paper. She needed to call the police and make a report. And she needed to clean up the remains of the coffee table. That was something she'd rather not have to explain.

But she wasn't doing anything until after coffee. The plaque hanging over her kitchen table back home summed it up nicely: Is there life before coffee? Everything was easier to face with an adequate shot of caffeine chugging through her veins.

Thirty minutes later, with her energy renewed and her hunger satisfied, she swung open the front door. Two uniformed police officers stood on the small porch. One she recognized immediately. Chief Branch hadn't changed. Well, he had changed, but in ways that just made him more... Branch. His paunch was bigger, his hair thinner, his condescending glance more obvious, and when she invited them in, his swagger was more pronounced than it had been eight years ago.

The other cop was young, early to mid-twenties, with sparkling blue eyes and dark brown hair that curled out from under his cap. He removed the cap, held it to his chest and nodded a greeting, accompanied by a familiar friendly smile.

"Alan?"

"Yep, it's me, in the flesh."

When she left eight years ago, he was a shy, scrawny fourteen-year-old who always had his nose in a book. She figured by now he'd be starting his doctorate, well on his way toward becoming a nuclear physicist or something equally brainy. Law enforcement was the last field she would have chosen for him.

But he looked the part. There was nothing shy or scrawny about him. Somewhere during his high school and college years, he had gained about six inches in height and an impressive amount in mass. The confidence he exuded would make people happy to place their safety in his hands. Especially some of the younger women of Harmony Grove.

"So the prodigal has returned."

Chief Branch's sarcastic tone doused some of the pleasure of seeing Alan again. Alan had always been nice. Chief Branch, not so much. He had ridden her hard, always watching for the slightest misstep, then had taken devious delight in throwing on the handcuffs and hauling her in.

She tried to match his look of disdain. "Don't worry. I'm not staying."

"Good. It's been nice and peaceful here with you gone."

She turned away and moved farther into the room. Branch still saw her as the troubled teen with a megasize chip on her shoulder. Well, she wasn't that person anymore. Maybe the chip was still there. But it was a lot smaller. She had grown up, learned some responsibility and taken charge of her life.

But the people of Harmony Grove wouldn't see it that way. In their eyes, she would always be trouble, unless she spent a lot of time proving otherwise. And that wasn't going to happen. She wouldn't be here long enough.

Branch's gaze circled the room. "So what happened?"

"I don't know. I arrived early this morning to find the whole house ransacked. I haven't seen any signs of forced entry." They probably came in the same way she did, through the slider. Anywhere else, there would be proof.

Branch eyed her suspiciously. "How did *you* get in? Oh, never mind, you're an old pro at breaking and entering."

She bristled at the condescending tone. That wasn't fair. Her own house didn't count. And she had broken into someone else's only twice. She didn't steal anything either time. That wasn't the reason she had done it. It was to prove she could. She never had been able to back down from a dare.

Alan stepped forward before she could respond. "Why don't I go ahead and see if I can lift some prints."

"That sounds good." She would deal with Alan and do her best to ignore Branch. "This room's not bad." If it weren't for the throw pillows littering the floor and some haphazard piles of DVDs that had been pulled from the entertainment center shelves, the area would look like any other living room on the street. That was where she had slept, with two of the throw pillows tucked under her head.

Alan dusted the entertainment center for prints then moved down the hall. When the doorways, doorknobs and dressers in the first bedroom had been dusted with the fine black powder, he moved into the master bedroom. Branch followed, watching Alan but not doing much himself. That was probably typical. He didn't look to be in good enough shape to do anything but supervise. The grunt work was probably beneath him anyway.

Alan swiveled his head toward her. "This might have been what they were looking for."

She walked over to where he knelt in the corner. A monitor, keyboard and mouse sat atop a small desk, the tower on the floor next to it. Someone had removed the tower's cover. She hadn't noticed it before. Of course, all she had done was give the room a cursory glance before heading out to pick up breakfast.

He turned back to his work and began brushing fine powder over the cover. "The hard drive is missing."

She crossed her arms and pursed her lips. Someone must have been awfully concerned about something Prissy had. A photo, maybe? Some kind of incriminating evidence? Sensitive information? "Where did my sister work?"

"Pappy's Pizzeria. She was a waitress."

A Lotus Exige on a waitress's pay? Not likely. Priscilla did more than wait tables—something someone was determined to keep secret.

Alan finished inside, then focused his attention on the open front door. Across the street, a familiar figure made his way down the wrought iron steps outside Yesteryear Antiques. Her pulse rate picked up a notch, and her stomach did a little flip. She put the brakes on both. He was just being neighborly. And if he had anything more in mind, she would put the brakes on that, too. She knew his type all too well.

Alan made his way around the exterior of the house as Shane crossed Main Street and started up the driveway. Branch lingered on the porch.

"You know," Branch said as soon as Alan was out of earshot, "Harmony Grove has done just fine without you all these years. So don't think you're going to come back here and stir up trouble, or life won't be pleasant for you."

She plastered on a phony smile as Shane stepped onto the porch beside Branch.

"She wouldn't dream of it."

Branch turned and took a stumbling step backward, mouth agape and jowls jiggling. "Who—who are you?"

"Shane Dalton." He was as composed as Branch was flustered. "And you are?"

Branch recovered almost immediately. "Chief Grady Branch." He emphasized the word *chief,* even seemed to bow up as he said it. "Are you a friend of this woman?"

"*This woman* is Jess Parker. And yes, as of two o'clock this morning, I'd like to think so. At least once she finished beating me up."

Branch looked from Shane to her and back to Shane, then opened his mouth and snapped it shut again before waddling away to find Alan. She pinched her lips against the burst of laughter charging up her throat. Just as Branch disappeared around the corner of the house, she lost the battle, and it bubbled over anyway.

"Thank you for that," she said, still laughing. "I'll cherish the memory of that look of stunned shock as long as I live."

"Glad I could oblige. It looks as if you've done something to tick off your chief of police."

"Not lately. I guess old grudges die hard."

"So have they found anything yet?"

"I'm not sure." She crossed her arms and leaned back against the closed front door. "Alan lifted lots of prints. Of course, they may all belong to Priscilla."

"That's always a possibility, especially if whoever did this wore gloves."

She nodded. "Her hard drive's gone. They took her computer apart to remove it."

"Hmm, she must have had some kind of dirt on somebody."

"And it must have weighed on her so heavy, she couldn't handle it anymore." Except that didn't sound like Priscilla. She was all about Priscilla and no one else. Not the type of person to feel remorse.

Movement in her peripheral vision drew her attention, and Jessica turned to see Mrs. Silverton making her way across the yard next door. A shaggy white dog lay cuddled in her arms, one of those yippy little ankle biters. The old lady had always loved Priscilla. Of course, everyone loved Priscilla.

Jessica straightened her shoulders while watery gray eyes swept over her. The judgment reserved for the teenage Jessica was absent. All the adult Jessica got was a thorough sizing up.

"Hello, dear. I'm so sorry about your sister."

"Thanks."

She dipped her head of curly white hair. "This

is Buttons, Priscilla's dog. She got him as a puppy five or six years ago."

Jessica looked down at the shaggy ball of fur studying her with those round, dark eyes, and her stomach tightened. She knew where this conversation was headed.

Mrs. Silverton brushed the hair out of Buttons's eyes, then ran her hand over his head and down his back. "When they found Priscilla, he was inside, sitting next to the bed, just waiting. Chief Branch brought him over here." She stopped petting him to cup his face in her hand. "I can tell he really misses her. He's done nothing but cry. I think he'd be happier in his own home."

Mrs. Silverton held Buttons out, clearly expecting Jessica to take him.

Wonderful. Not only did she have to dispose of Priscilla's things, now she was stuck finding a home for her dog. Keeping him was out of the question. She wasn't the nurturing type. If she ever decided to have a pet, it would be a cat. Or a bird. Dogs were too needy.

But Buttons wasn't Mrs. Silverton's responsibility. He was *hers.* Just like everything else Prissy had dumped in her lap.

She relieved the old lady of her burden and took possession of the little white fur ball. A now *quivering* fur ball. Great. Buttons was one of those yippy, *nervous* little ankle biters. Definitely high maintenance.

She turned to go inside as Branch and Alan came back around the front of the house.

"We're finished," Branch said. "We'll let you know if we find out anything."

Once inside, she set Buttons on the floor, then cast the mutt a disparaging glance. "Never say things can't get any worse, because they always can."

"Pet ownership isn't so bad." Shane squatted and offered the back of his hand. Buttons eyed him cautiously but didn't approach.

"If it's not so bad, then you take him."

"Can't. I move around too much. Not stable enough for a pet."

Yep, wild and carefree. She had him pegged right.

Shane stood and clapped his hands together. "Well, where would you like to start?"

She cocked one brow at him. In the light of a new day, she was second-guessing her decision to accept his help. Too many offers came with strings attached. She crossed her arms in front of her. "You know, you don't need to do this. I can handle it."

"I'm sure you can. But think how much more fun it'll be with me here." He flashed her a goofy grin.

She didn't take the bait. "Why are you offering your help? I can't pay you."

"And I wouldn't let you. I already told you. I'm being neighborly. Isn't that what people in small towns do?"

She studied him a couple beats more, then turned

and strode toward the kitchen. She really could use the help. "We'll start here." She needed to be able to cook. Even a fast-food diet was too expensive for her budget.

She took a stack of pans from Shane and squatted in front of one of the lower cabinets. "So what brings you to Harmony Grove?"

"Just looking for a change of scenery."

She slid the pans onto the bottom shelf and reached for another stack Shane had ready. "If you're looking for scenery, I would think you'd go for the beach. Or the mountains."

"Every locale has its own beauty. I'd say this is a good place to be in January. It's cold now, but give it a couple of days, and it'll be back up in the high seventies."

She nodded and crawled to the next cabinet. Maybe by lunchtime, they could have the kitchen put back together. Then the living room would be a breeze. The bedrooms were another story. Maybe she'd use the opportunity to get rid of a bunch of stuff. She believed in living simply. Priscilla obviously hadn't.

Shane handed her a set of Pyrex dishes and straightened to lean back against the cabinet. "Were you and your sister ever close?"

She slanted a glance at him. "Maybe for five minutes, when she first came home from the hospital." Her flippant tone held an underlying thread of bitterness. "Before that, my stepdad sort of tolerated me. Once Priscilla came along, I became the red-headed stepchild that nobody wanted. Prissy could do no wrong, and it didn't take her long to figure that out. She was constantly doing stuff and blaming it on me. Finally I decided if I was going to keep receiving the punishment, I might as well do the deed."

"I'm sorry you had to go through all that."

The tenderness in his voice caught her off guard. So did the sympathy in his eyes. Nobody had ever looked at her like that. Then again, she usually kept her past to herself. But there was something about being back in Harmony Grove, in the house where she grew up, surrounded by all the things she thought she'd never see again. It was making her soft.

She shrugged. "I turned out all right." Relatively speaking. *Better than Pris.*

As he handed her the last casserole dish, his phone rang, and he pressed it to his ear. "Hold on a second, will you, Ross?" He motioned toward the phone with his other hand. "I've got to take this call. I'll be back shortly."

"No problem. I need to make an appointment with an attorney. I doubt my sister had a will."

He turned and disappeared through the living room and out the front door. He obviously didn't want her to hear his side of the conversation. Regardless of what he said about the scenery, something told her this Shane Dalton was in Harmony

Grove for more than cow pastures, pine trees and palmettos. He seemed harmless enough. But frankly, she didn't have a whole lot of confidence in her ability to judge men's characters.

Especially lately.

"Have you got something for me?"

"I do." Shane's supervisor's bass voice boomed through the line. "Are you at your computer?"

"I will be in a minute." He jogged up the steps, taking them two at a time. "Okay," he said, once the system was booted up. "I'm on. Send it through."

A couple of clicks later, banking records filled the screen. "This is Priscilla Parker's account?"

"It is."

He leaned forward, scrolling backward through the entries. "Deposits of around two thousand a week. All the way back to the beginning of November."

"Yep, ten weeks worth."

Shane finished scrolling and leaned back in his chair. "So what did she do for a living?"

"She was a waitress at a local pizza joint, Pappy's Pizzeria. Been there for two years. Unless she suddenly acquired some wealthy customers who were great tippers, I would say she had her hands in something a little more lucrative than waitressing."

"What kind of background does she have?"

"Squeaky clean. Not even a speeding ticket."

Shane smiled wryly. "That just means she hasn't

been caught." After all, she was young, had just celebrated her twenty-first birthday. She was a pretty girl. He had seen her photo on the end table in the Parker living room.

The Parker sisters looked nothing alike. Besides the obvious difference in hair color, Jess's eyes were a rich, deep brown, while Priscilla's had been blue—he would call them *ice-blue*—with a coldness that came through even in the photo. Priscilla had possessed almost wispy features that needed enhancement with makeup, whereas Jessica's high cheekbones, deep-set eyes and angled jaw gave her an almost exotic beauty.

And Jessica was very much alive. Priscilla wasn't. Suicides were always sad. Even more so when someone had her whole life ahead of her. Except this one was starting to smell an awful lot like murder.

"Any details on her death?"

"Yeah," Ross answered. "Looks as if she overdosed on oxycodone. I've got a police report and an autopsy report. I'll send them through. They estimate her time of death at around 12:30 a.m., but she wasn't found until midafternoon the following day when she didn't show up for work. The house was locked up tight, and when the police broke in, she was lying in bed in her PJs. There was a syringe beside her, along with the empty pill bottle, and a mortar and pestle on the nightstand."

"She crushed and injected them?"

"Yep. Shooting that mess up gives them a faster and better high. Or in this case, a quick, sure death. The autopsy report shows a needle mark in her left arm, just below the bend of the elbow."

Shane hit print and watched the pages drop into the tray. "Anything else interesting?"

"Yeah. She had some faint bruising on her upper arms and wrists, as if someone had manhandled her a bit. Which makes me wonder if she didn't have some help injecting that lethal dose. Or maybe the bruises are nothing more than the marks of a rough boyfriend."

"Hmm, that raises some serious questions." Especially in light of everything else he had learned.

"Yeah, it should. But based on the evidence, the medical examiner ruled it a suicide. The house was locked up tight and her prints were all over the bottle and the mortar and pestle, with some partials taken from the syringe. I'd be interested in seeing how the local police are handling it."

"Yeah, me, too." He had met the local police, at least the chief, and he wasn't impressed. "Sometime between her death and when I got there, the house was ransacked. So someone's after something."

"You've been inside?"

"Oh, yeah, I was inside." He rose from the chair and rubbed his bruised ribs. "So was Priscilla Parker's sister. I saw her breaking in, and when I went to investigate, she got a wee bit defensive."

Ross's throaty chuckle flowed through the phone. "Sounds as if she might have whooped up on you."

"The woman's a second-degree black belt." He moved to the window where he had an unobstructed view of the front and one side of the Parker place. Jessica was inside, probably on the phone securing her appointment. He intended to keep her close. Because the more he learned, the more convinced he was that there was foul play. And Jessica Parker was just bold enough to put herself right in the middle of it. If she wasn't already there.

He moved away from the window and strode across the room. The apartment was small, but its proximity to Jessica made it perfect for his purposes. The front half consisted of a single large room containing a kitchen, eating area and living room. The bedroom and bath were in the back.

"Do me a favor." He eased onto the couch and propped his feet on the coffee table. "I need you to run Priscilla Parker's tag, one of those vanity plates, PRIS 92. It's on a Lotus Exige, which is way out of reach on a waitress's pay. See what you can find out about the purchase."

"Will do."

"And how about checking out this sister for me. The name's Jess, probably short for Jessica." He still didn't know what to think of her. The tough air, defensive stance and guarded eyes hinted that her record may not be as spotless as her little sister's. If Jess had some possible involvement in his drug case or Priscilla Parker's apparent suicide, he needed to know. In the meantime, he wasn't going to be swayed by her exotic good looks or her sad childhood.

"Anyone else?"

"Yeah, Grady Branch, the chief of police."

"Think you might have a dirty cop?"

"Probably not." Conceited? Yes. Condescending? Definitely. But dirty? Not likely. Too much effort for him. But it never hurt to check.

He disconnected the call and let his head rest against the back of the couch. Across the room, a large plate glass window framed a small brick church and invited in the morning sunshine. The sign out front read Cornerstone Community Church. He couldn't see it from his vantage point on the second floor, but he had read it earlier, along with the service times. Maybe Sunday he would go.

Sometimes he got to attend church. Usually he didn't. It just depended on the assignment. When he was trying to blend with the bad guys, it was out of the question. Unless the bad guys attended. Occasionally they did.

He let out a wistful sigh. That was something he missed, being active in the church in Southern Ohio where he had grown up, worshiping with people he had known all his life, enjoying monthly dinners on the grounds with Tricia Duncan's homemade mac and cheese and old Mrs. Wilson's blackberry cobbler. Watching services on TV, alone in an empty motel room or apartment, just wasn't the same. But that was how he spent far too many of his Sunday mornings.

That fellowship with other Christians was just one of the things he had given up when he left the local police force to join the Bureau. There were others. Sleeping in his own bed three hundred fifty nights of every year. Getting together with lifelong friends. Having a social life that was the real deal.

But his career choice had its advantages, too. The schedule kept him from dwelling too much on past mistakes. He got to see places he would otherwise never visit. He had met more people in the past two years than he had in the prior ten. And always at the end of an assignment, he could walk away, because he was never in the same place long enough to form any real emotional bonds.

Never again would his affections put another person's life in danger. Never again would someone close to him pay the ultimate price for his drive to see justice done.

And that was worth everything he had given up.

THREE

Jessica stood in front of the bank of elevators at the county courthouse, clutching the folded sheet of notebook paper. She had retained a probate attorney, Harmony Grove's own Mark Downing. Mark requested an emergency hearing, and the hearing had been granted. Super fast. He said he pulled some strings. That was the good news.

Her eyes dropped to the paper and scanned the words she had scrawled there yesterday, "Wednesday, 2:30, Judge Daniel Peterson, Courtroom 7B."

And that was the bad news.

Of all the judges in Polk County, why did she have to get stuck with Peterson? He was a juvenile judge. At least he used to be. Mark said he transferred out five years ago. Hopefully he wouldn't hold the past against her. Because he would definitely remember her. She had appeared in his courtroom too many times.

The bell dinged and the elevator doors opened, beckoning her in. As soon as she stepped off on the seventh floor, Mark met her. When she left home as a troubled teen, he was in his second year of community college. Now she was back, and he had a J.D. after his name. The Harmony Grove attorney was fine. The Harmony Grove judge she could do without. Maybe those were the strings Mark had referred to.

Judge Peterson read the pleadings without a flicker of recognition in his steel-gray eyes. Then he invited Mark to speak.

"Your Honor, in view of the fact that Priscilla Parker left no will, we are requesting that you appoint her sister, Jessica Parker, to be executor of the estate and give her access to all of Priscilla's accounts."

Judge Peterson's gaze raked her from head to toe. Oh, yeah. He remembered her. There was no doubt. She squared her shoulders. She wasn't coming before him as a rebellious teenager, in trouble yet again. She was presenting as a responsible woman. Her whole appearance screamed *professional,* from the well-fitting charcoal blazer to the red silk blouse underneath, to the matching skirt whose hem, when she was standing, rested a modest three inches above her knees.

"Miss Parker, approach the bench."

She rose from the chair and walked to the front. "Yes, Your Honor?"

"Has next of kin been notified?"

"Your Honor, I *am* next of kin."

"What about your mother?"

She resisted the urge to roll her eyes. Her first day back, she learned that her mother had put the house in Priscilla's name and taken off the weekend Priscilla turned eighteen. Everyone in town knew, which meant Peterson did, too. "No one has seen or heard from my mother in over three years."

"Well, I'm going to have to deliberate on it. Someone should try harder to locate her. I'll notify Mr. Downing here of my decision."

Maybe arguing with the judge wasn't a good idea. But in Harmony Grove, she wasn't known for making smart decisions. "Your Honor, they've already tried. If there had been any way to reach her, they would never have called me. I need access to Priscilla's accounts. There are bills to be paid. I know for a fact there's a mortgage on the house. And I'm sure she didn't pay cash for that fancy sports car."

"Well, Miss Parker, these things take time. Nothing moves fast in the legal system. Your best bet is to go back to wherever home is, and Mr. Downing will let you know when there's any change." He declared the hearing adjourned, rose from the bench and walked away.

She stared after the black-robed figure, jaw agape. He was holding her past against her, abusing his position of power to make her pay for deeds she had committed a decade earlier. She snapped her mouth closed and turned accusing eyes on Mark.

"There was no reason for him to not grant that

request. How am I supposed to pay Prissy's bills without access to her accounts?"

Mark cast a nervous glance at the bailiff and court reporter, then put an arm across her shoulders to guide her from the room. "Let's talk outside."

She nodded and bit her tongue. At least Prissy's final expenses were covered by a small life insurance policy she had through Pappy's. She learned that yesterday. Pappy and Edith DelRoss had even made the arrangements. The funeral would be at three Saturday afternoon, and she didn't have to do a thing.

Jess followed Mark through a door downstairs that led to a covered patio area. Courthouse employees and visitors sat around tables taking afternoon smoke breaks. She held her silence a moment longer and moved toward the crosswalk. "Okay," she said, stepping into the January sunshine, "we're outside now." She stopped at the edge of Church Street, which separated the courthouse from the parking lots, and jabbed an index finger into his chest. "You give me one good reason why he couldn't grant my request."

"I *am* a little surprised. I thought it would be pretty cut and dry. But he has a point about your mother."

"That's hogwash. He knows full well that my mother can't be found. She didn't exactly leave a forwarding address. He's just being difficult because it's me." She turned and began stalking toward the parking lot. "What did I ever do to him? Sure, I kept winding up in his courtroom. But that was his job. Nothing to hold a personal grudge for."

"Well, there was the time you and my sister egged his house."

His reminder brought a grimace. "Oh, yeah."

He rested a hand on her shoulder. Mark obviously didn't hold the past against her. Of course, his sister, Jasmine, was usually her partner in crime. It was never anything serious, just stupid stuff like putting soap in the fountain downtown so that by morning half the park was covered in a layer of fluffy white suds, or catching a bunch of tree frogs and sneaking them into old Ms. Willoughby's classroom. Besides, Mark hadn't been a model child himself.

He gave her shoulder a squeeze. "Give it a couple of weeks. My guess is this will all be straightened out long before the first bill goes into collection."

"All right, two weeks."

He headed off toward where he had parked some distance away, and she continued to her car. Regardless of what Mark said, Judge Peterson was keeping her from her sister's records just to be difficult.

Or maybe there was something he didn't want her to see.

What had Priscilla gotten mixed up in? What did she have that someone had tried so hard to find? After a full day of sorting, she didn't know any more than she had before. Other than the missing hard drive, nothing she had encountered hinted at anything more sinister than a reluctance to throw things away. She and Shane had packed up box after box of the normal accessories of life—Priscilla's life, Mom's life, even Jessica's own.

Eight years had passed, but her things were all still there—school yearbooks, favorite stuffed animals, clothes and shoes that she had left behind in her hasty escape from Harmony Grove. It had probably been packed up for years, until being dumped on the floor with all the other stuff. But the fact that Priscilla hadn't gotten rid of it spoke volumes. Maybe she felt some sentimental attachment to the things that had belonged to her older sister. Or maybe she had always held out hope that the wayward sister would eventually return.

Yeah, right. Those were nice thoughts. But she knew Priscilla. More than likely she had just never gotten around to getting rid of the stuff.

She held up her key fob and pressed the unlock button, listening for the telltale beep. Four spaces down, the little green Bug sat sandwiched between two SUVs. She opened the driver door and slid into the seat. Her trip to Bartow hadn't accomplished anything she had hoped. She still didn't know what bills Priscilla owed and had no way to pay them if she did.

But it wasn't a wasted trip. She came away with a strong suspicion that there was more to her sister's suicide than she had initially thought. Judge Peterson didn't want her having access to Priscilla's information. He even told her to leave Harmony Grove and go back to Miami.

Well, she wasn't going. Something stank, and she wasn't giving up until she found out what. She could wait it out indefinitely. She didn't have a job to go back to anyway. Her overbearing, unreasonable boss had told her to be back in forty-eight hours, or not to bother coming back. She was taking his threat to heart. No great loss. It was just one more in a series of dead-end jobs she had had no choice but to accept since her decorating business went belly-up eight months ago.

And her apartment? She liked where she lived. But with less income, it was just a matter of time until she would have to let it go. She was paid through the end of January. Her lease ended six months ago, and she had been on month-to-month ever since. With no notice, she wouldn't get her security deposit back, but c'est la vie.

As she pulled onto Broadway, church bells sounded, drawing her attention to the stately white building on her right, its tall steeple topped with a metal cross. Churches were nice to look at. But that was about all. People came to do their duty and pay homage to a God who neither saw nor cared about the petty struggles of man.

Her gaze fell on the sign out front, where black letters proclaimed their message of hope—Seek God While He May Be Found.

She emitted an unladylike snort. Why? What did

God ever do for her? He didn't stop father number one from leaving. Or make father number two give her the time of day. Or protect her from father number three.

Doesn't look as if He did a whole lot for Pris, either.

Shane watched the Volkswagen screech to a stop in the driveway across the street, Jess at the wheel. As soon as she stepped from the vehicle, she slammed the car door and charged toward the house with determined steps. Evidently her trip to court hadn't gone well.

By the time he made it downstairs and across the street, she was already inside. He rang the bell, and the door swung inward. Jess stood framed in the opening, signature form-fitting jeans and biker boots gone. Instead, she wore a simple straight skirt and matching jacket with a modest pair of pumps. The blazer and skirt hugged her curves as if they were custom-made for her body. But the whole look was so not Jess. At least not the tough, sassy-chic Jess he had come to know over the past three days.

"You look like a lawyer. Something tells me that wasn't pulled together from your current wardrobe."

She flashed him a crooked grin. "How did you guess? No, I'm afraid this entailed raiding Prissy's closet. I wanted to look professional. Although I can't say it did any good."

"I take it things didn't go well."

"Not at all. I got Judge Peterson." She frowned up at him. "He was the juvenile court judge that I kept winding up in front of as a teenager. Guess what? He doesn't do juvie anymore."

That shouldn't make a difference. Judges were supposed to be impartial. Of course, he knew better. "So what happened?"

"He isn't making me executor of my sister's estate or giving me access to any of her accounts. He says they need to try to find my mother."

"But no one knows where she is."

"My point exactly." She kicked off her shoes and plopped down on the couch. Buttons jumped up next to her and snuggled against her thigh. "Believe me, I know these people. Contacting me was a last resort. But he's insisting on going through the motions. Meanwhile, I'm supposed to keep her bills paid by pulling money out of thin air." She waved her arm for emphasis, then dropped it to rest on the dog's back.

"You think he's doing that just to be difficult?"

"Yes and no. I think he's enjoying hampering me at every turn, but I also believe there's something he doesn't want me to see."

He had come to the same conclusion. "What do you mean?"

"My sister wasn't the Goody Two-shoes she always pretended to be. Good law-abiding citizens don't get their houses ransacked. I'm guessing there's something suspicious in her banking or other records."

Yes, there was, and he had that something right across the street. Maybe eventually he could share it with her.

She heaved a sigh. "I guess I'm going to be staying here longer than I planned. I *am* going to get to the bottom of this. I refuse to be run off by Judge Peterson or Chief Branch." The stubborn determination in her eyes set off all kinds of alarms in his head. Just what he needed, an overzealous sister charging blindly into danger and getting them both hurt.

He sank down onto the couch next to her. "You probably need to take it easy and let the police do their job."

The irreverent snort told him exactly what she thought of his suggestion. "With what you saw of Chief Branch this morning, do you really believe that's going to happen?" She continued without waiting for a response. "So I'm staying. That means I'm going to have to find a job."

"Any leads?"

"I haven't started looking yet."

"What do you do?"

She frowned. "I can tell you what I *did* easier than I can tell you what I *do*. I ran a special-events decorating company—weddings, conventions, parties, lots of bar and bat mitzvahs, quince parties. It was great. Until the bottom fell out."

"Making a business succeed in this economy can be quite a challenge."

"Oh, my business was handling the economy just fine. What it couldn't survive was the crooked business partner."

"I'm sorry to hear that." The rough life she had had as a child evidently hadn't gotten a whole lot easier.

She shrugged off his concern and raised her chin, showing a strength he admired. "I'll get back on my feet. Meanwhile, I'm taking whatever I can get that'll pay the bills. Especially since I seem to have now acquired my sister's."

He nodded thoughtfully. She was experiencing some serious financial issues, problems that started eight months ago. And her sister had apparently come into money, judging from her checking-account deposits and the drool-worthy ride sitting in the driveway. It was looking as if Jess had a lot to gain from her sister's death. If she could get her hands on the money.

She swiveled her head to look at him directly. "What about you? You never did tell me what kind of work you do."

"I'm writing a book." That was his pat answer if he didn't already have a job assignment. It left his options wide-open. And it was sort of true. He had an idea. And notes. Lots of notes. Maybe one day he would tackle it seriously.

"What's it about?"

"I can't tell you. Well, I could, but then I'd have to kill you."

She gave him a quirky grin. "Afraid I'll steal your idea?"

"You never know."

"I bet it's a spy novel." She narrowed her gaze to study him, but remnants of the grin lingered. "You look like a James Bond kind of guy. I'm guessing you'd be into all the intrigue and espionage."

He raised his brows, unease nibbling at the edges of his mind. There was no way she could suspect he was an agent. Of course, he did pull a gun on her within moments of meeting her. But that didn't mean anything. A lot of guys packed heat. "Why do you say that?"

"Just a guess. I mean, isn't that what reading is all about? Escape from everyday life?" She pushed herself up from the couch. "Speaking of everyday life, I was so put out with Judge Peterson when I got home, I forgot to bring in the mail."

"I'll get it for you."

He returned a minute later with a small stack, most of which looked like junk mail. As soon as she took it from him, she tossed sales flyers on the end table. One by one, envelopes joined the sloppy pile. She stopped at one labeled Florida Gun School and tore open the seal. While she removed and unfolded the single page, he stood next to her, looking down at what she held.

Priscilla had enrolled in a weapons-training

class—the NRA Certified Basic Pistol Shooting Course, according to the letter. And she had missed the first class. The dates and location of the next course followed, with instructions to call and re-schedule.

Jess dropped her hands to her side and looked up at him, accusation in her gaze. "You tell me why someone with plans to commit suicide would enroll in a pistol-shooting course." She tossed the letter on the table with the other mail and started to pace. "If she bought a gun with plans to kill herself, she would have used it."

"Maybe she never got the money together to buy the gun. Or maybe she changed her mind. You have to admit, overdosing is a whole lot less messy."

She stopped her pacing long enough to nail him with a withering glare. "Don't give me that. No one enrolls in a ten-hour shooting course to figure out how to kill herself. I mean, it's not that diffi-cult. You point it here—" she put a finger to her temple then in her mouth "—or here, and you pull the trigger."

She spun away from him and stalked off down the hall.

"Where are you going?"

"I'm betting there's a gun back here somewhere. And I guarantee you she bought it to protect her-self."

When he reached the doorway of the master bed-room, she was on her knees in front of the closet, clothes and objects flying. He leaned back against the doorjamb, unwilling to enter the room. Even Buttons was maintaining a safe distance. If she *was* somehow involved in her sister's death, she was putting on a pretty convincing performance.

After several minutes of arranging and rearranging the mess covering the floor, she stood up clutching a brown leather case. "See, I told you." She unsnapped the strap across the top, gripped the wooden handle and removed a pistol. "This is a gun. She bought it to protect herself. Does that sound like someone who planned to down a bottle of pills?"

She was right. It was a gun. It looked like a thirty-eight, but the way she was waving it around, he wasn't sure. He tensed and charged into the room, taking it from her. "Watch out. It could be loaded."

"Someone killed her, Shane."

She looked up at him, eyes pleading with him to believe her. The entreaty in her gaze threatened to shatter the last of his doubt, and a seed of tension sprouted in his gut. He didn't like where this was headed. If she believed there was foul play, she would be a one-woman vigilante team, forging ahead with unstoppable zeal, determined to bring her sister's killer to justice.

He draped an arm across her shoulders. A good seven or eight inches shorter than he was, she fit there perfectly. A sudden sense of protectiveness surged through him, taking him aback. Maybe it was her small stature. Or the knowledge that, with her sister gone and her mom having disappeared, she was all alone. Whatever it was, it wasn't from any misguided notion that she actually needed him. Because nothing about Jess was weak or needy.

"You don't know that," he said, tone filled with a conviction he didn't feel. "Everything points to suicide. The house was locked up tight, and her prints were all over everything."

"But how do you explain the gun and the weapons class?" Suddenly she pulled away, gaze narrowed, full of suspicion. "Wait, how did you know that?"

Dread settled over him, lining his stomach with lead. What was wrong with him? He was losing his edge. Without thinking, he had blurted something he shouldn't have known. "It's common knowledge. It's all over town." At least he hoped it was.

He released a sigh and wrapped an arm around her again. "Let it go, Jess. I know you want to vindicate your sister. But if you're right, if there was foul play and you keep pushing, you could be next. Let the police take care of it." *Let me take care of it.* Of course, she would be more willing to do that if she knew who he was. But he was a long way from trusting her enough to blow his cover.

She studied him in silence, then gave a brief nod and walked from the room.

And he didn't believe it for a minute. He shook

his head and followed her down the hall. Bold, beautiful, impetuous Jess.

If only he could keep her from getting herself killed.

FOUR

BethAnn's Fabrics and Crafts.

Jessica eyed the sign hanging over the shop nestled between Dani's Bakery and Remarkable Repeats Consignment Shoppe. BethAnn Thomas had left Harmony Grove long before she did, but how many BethAnns could there be?

She swung the glass door open and stepped inside as a woman dropped a bolt of checkered fabric onto a cutting table. Corkscrew curls bobbed as she worked, and even in profile, her smile was obvious. Yep, definitely BethAnn Thomas. She was doing well—owner of her own business and evidently married. At least, she was sporting a pretty good-size baby bump.

Jessica eased the door shut behind her. The main task on today's agenda was talking to the people of Harmony Grove. She and Shane had made headway on the work at the house but didn't know any more than when they started. At least nothing of value. They learned that Priscilla liked expensive clothes, romantic suspense books and a variety of movies. And she was sloppy with paperwork. Her check register was horribly out of date, and the stacks of bills sitting on the computer desk showed no indication of whether they had been paid. Nothing in the whole place hinted at who might have wanted to see her dead.

BethAnn looked up as she approached and offered her a sympathetic smile. "I'm so sorry about your sister. It was such a shock." She laid the scissors down and stepped out from behind the table to put a comforting hand on her arm. "Melissa and I had dinner at Pappy's the night before this happened, and she waited on us. She seemed fine."

"I know. This is so uncharacteristic of the Priscilla I knew." Of course, the Priscilla she knew was a thirteen-year-old child. But she wouldn't mention that. She ran her hand over the smooth laminate surface of the table and looked back at BethAnn. "I'm hoping someone might be able to shed some light on what might have happened."

The click of heels against the vinyl-tile floor cut into their conversation. "Okay, this is it."

Jessica didn't need to turn to know who approached. That shrill voice could belong to only one person. Carolyn Platt walked toward them carrying two bolts of fabric, platinum curls piled atop her head. Penciled-on eyebrows disappeared beneath starched bangs, and her eyes filled with interest.

"Jessica? I figured you would be coming back. I wouldn't have recognized you otherwise."

Jessica nodded a greeting. Carolyn prided herself on knowing everyone's business. It was what she lived for. Over the years, the Parkers had been the subject of quite a bit of Carolyn gossip.

"I'm back for now." She shook her head. "I just can't imagine Priscilla doing this."

Carolyn dropped the two bolts onto the counter. "A yard and a half of each."

While BethAnn cut the fabric, Carolyn continued with an eagerness she wasn't able to hide. "It *is* hard to comprehend. But she had some issues. I heard she was seeing Dr. Stonington." She looked around, as if afraid someone might overhear, then lowered her voice. "He's a psychiatrist."

Jessica nodded. She had known it would be easy to get Carolyn started. "Any idea why?"

"No, but I bet Alexis would know something. They've been best friends for years."

Yeah, since second grade. Lexi was sweet, like Priscilla. But with Lexi, it wasn't an act.

"Thanks. I'll go talk to her."

BethAnn came out from behind the counter and headed toward the cash register. Instead of following, Carolyn put a hand on Jessica's arm. "That's not all. A few months ago, she got a new boyfriend, and after that, she seemed…I don't know, different."

"Different, like how?"

"Oh, not as friendly anymore. As if she was too

good for the rest of us. She started showing up around town with fancy new clothes, you know, designer stuff. I guess Hammy was buying it for her. He's the one who bought her that expensive sports car. Since the old man died, Hammy's half owner of Driggers Porcelain, so I guess he can afford it."

She raised her brows. "Priscilla was dating Hammy Driggers?"

Carolyn bobbed her head. "A pretty unlikely match. That boy's always in trouble."

That *boy* would be twenty-eight now. And yes, he was trouble, always had been.

"Well," Carolyn said, "I think she's ready to check me out."

Jessica waited for Carolyn to pay for her purchase and leave. There was one more thing she wanted to ask BethAnn. And it had nothing to do with Priscilla. The door swung shut, leaving them alone.

"You wouldn't happen to be looking for help, would you?"

"Actually, I was going to put a sign in the window next week." She rested a hand on her swollen belly. "As you can see, I'm less than a month away from needing to take time off."

When Jessica walked out ten minutes later, it was with instructions to be there at nine Monday morning. Securing a job had been easier than expected, especially with her reputation in Harmony Grove. But BethAnn was quick to forgive past wrongs. And those last three jobs she hated gave her the experience she needed. Luck was with her for a change. It was almost like divine intervention.

Yeah, right. God didn't acknowledge her, and she didn't acknowledge Him.

She slid into the little green Bug and headed for the edge of town. According to BethAnn, Lexi was in her second year at Polk State College and still lived at home. Jessica didn't need directions. She had dropped Prissy off at the Simmons residence dozens of times. Ever since getting her license, and even before, she played taxi driver when her mom was too soused to get behind the wheel. Her underage driving started between father number two and father number three.

When she rang the bell at the familiar ranch-style home, Lexi opened the door. "Jessie? Is that you?"

Okay, she hadn't changed *that* much. Her hair was shorter, she had dropped the extra twenty pounds that had plagued her through high school and she had ditched the extreme makeup. But other than that...

Before she had a chance to respond, Lexi wrapped her in a spontaneous hug. When she finally released her, she looked ready to burst into tears.

"I still can't believe it." Her voice broke, and Jessica silently pleaded with her to hold it together. She wasn't good with sobbing females.

"Can I come in?"

"Sure." Lexi led her into the living room, motioned for her to sit, then took a place on the adjacent love seat.

Jessica drew in a deep breath, unsure where to begin. "You probably know Prissy and I hadn't spoken since I left."

Lexi nodded.

"I was angry. I had snuck out, and she squealed on me. When I crawled back through my bedroom window, Buck was waiting for me and beat me within an inch of my life."

"Prissy didn't mean for that to happen. She felt really bad about it afterward."

Jessica gave her a wry smile. "I thought she lived for the thrill of getting me in trouble."

"It was more to make herself look good. She always wanted to be the favorite."

"I'd say she succeeded."

"She didn't think so."

No, she probably didn't. If Prissy thought less love for Jess would mean more love for her, she was wrong. Love didn't live in their house, period. The Parker home defined the word *dysfunctional.*

Lexi looked down at her hands clasped in her lap and lowered her voice. "Things weren't easy for her after you left."

Jessica almost laughed, but something in Lexi's tone stopped her. "I can't imagine Buck beating *her* to a pulp. She was too much of a Goody Two-shoes to get into any real trouble."

"No, he never beat her."

Jessica sat unmoving, a sense of foreboding trickling over her. Lexi's words hung in the air between them, heavy with meaning, hinting at other, more horrific words she was unwilling to voice.

"What?" she prodded. "What did he do to her?"

Lexi shook her head. "She made me promise not to tell."

"He touched her, didn't he?"

Lexi looked at her and nodded. Tears pooled against her lower lashes but didn't overflow. "After you left, he started coming into her room when your mom was passed out drunk. He said if she told anyone, he'd hurt her the same way he hurt you."

Jessica closed her eyes, nausea gripping her. Even with all the grief Priscilla had caused her, she didn't deserve that. No one did. "Did she try to tell anyone? Did *you* tell anyone?"

"I didn't know. Prissy just told me a few months ago. She tried to tell your mom back then, but she didn't believe her, just told her to keep her mouth shut. So Prissy didn't think anyone else would believe her, either. Finally, she put a knife to his throat and told him if he touched her again she would kill him in his sleep. He left a week later. She was seventeen."

Seventeen. Four long years.

Jessica stood and strode toward the door. She needed fresh air. No, what she needed was somewhere to throw up.

She should have been there. What were a few

beatings? She should have toughed it out and stayed to protect her younger sister. Instead, she had run away and left her to endure four years of the worst kind of abuse. No wonder Priscilla killed herself.

Or maybe Buck killed her to keep her quiet. Maybe she had threatened to finally tell.

She stopped in the doorway and turned to face Lexi. "Do you know if she had any contact with him after that? Especially recently?"

"Not that she mentioned."

There was one other person who might have information. "Was she getting any kind of professional help, a psychiatrist, a counselor or anything?"

"No. Several months ago, she went to a psychiatrist and got a prescription for some antidepressants, but she didn't like the way they made her feel. So she stopped taking them. She never went back."

Jessica nodded. "Carolyn Platt told me Prissy was dating Hammy."

"Yeah. They started dating last July." She drew her brows together and pursed her lips. "It was kind of strange, actually."

"How so?"

"I don't know, it just seemed one-sided. He was really smitten with her. You could tell. But she was kind of flippant, as if she could take him or leave him. She didn't act like someone in love. I think she was using him more than anything."

"How did they get along?"

"They seemed to get along fine. Except the day

before she died. That night, she stopped by my house after work. She was upset, so we went for a ride. She told me they had had a fight. She wouldn't tell me what it was about, just that she had made him really mad."

"Do you think he would have done anything to hurt her?"

Lexi shook her head. "I can't imagine he would. Like I said, he was crazy about her. But after that fight, she seemed really agitated. I knew she wasn't herself, because she left her phone in my car. And she was *never* separated from her new iPhone."

Jessica stepped out the door and onto the porch. "If you think of anything I might find interesting, call me. I'll give you my cell number."

Although Lexi didn't think Hammy would hurt Prissy, the fact remained that they had had a big blowout the day before she died. But Hammy wasn't at the top of her list.

Buck was.

With Prissy gone, he would never be tried for his other crimes. But if he was guilty of murder, she would do everything in her power to see justice done.

Shane walked between the red Lotus and the little green Bug, a DVD stuffed into the pocket of his jacket. The Lotus, of course, hadn't moved. The Bug had been gone since early morning, having returned only forty-five minutes ago. Jess hadn't told him what she had planned, just that she was going to be out all day.

Before he reached the small porch, the front door swung open and she stepped out. Blue jeans disappeared into boots similar to the ones he had experienced on first meeting her, except in brown. A tan jacket wrapped her upper body, its belt cinched tightly around her waist. She looked good. Of course, she always looked good.

He jerked his gaze back to her face. "Leaving again so soon?"

"Oh, hi." She pulled the door shut behind her but didn't step off the porch. "I'm going to see someone. If he's home."

If *he's* home. Maybe she was headed out to see a former flame. A hollowness in his chest accompanied the thought, and he chided himself. Whoever she saw, it was none of his concern.

He patted his jacket pocket. "I stopped by the video store and picked up a movie. But I guess you're busy." He wasn't quite able to keep the disappointment out of his voice. Another evening alone. And alone was getting old. Yeah, that was it. That hollowness was disappointment. If she rekindled an old romance, he would be spending lots of evenings alone.

She flashed him an apologetic smile. "Can I take a rain check?"

"Sure. So how was your day?"

"Productive." The smile broadened. "I landed a job. I start Monday."

"Congratulations. You must be heading out to celebrate."

"No celebrations tonight."

Her somber tone laid to rest his earlier thoughts of reigniting old sparks. He ignored the sense of relief that shot through him. Whether Jess was involved with someone made no difference to him one way or the other. Sure, he was attracted to her. But he had no intention of acting on it. Men in his line of work had no business making romantic commitments. Because men in his line of work had enemies. And sometimes retaliatory bullets found the wrong target.

He shook off the disconcerting thoughts. "So where are you headed?"

"I'm paying Hammy Driggers a visit. Priscilla's boyfriend."

"You think he might know something about why Priscilla killed herself?"

"Or was murdered."

Great. She hadn't let it go. "Mind if I tag along?"

"I prefer to work alone." She brushed past him to step down off the porch and saunter toward her car.

He fell in beside her. "And I prefer to know you're not charging in making accusations that are going to get you killed."

"You don't have much confidence in me, do

you?" She opened the door of the Bug and slid into the driver's seat.

"Come on, Jess. Let me go with you. If there's anything to learn, two heads are better than one. And if you're right and there's any danger, we can back each other up."

She studied him, those dark eyes unreadable as usual. Finally she tilted her head toward the passenger's side. "Get in."

He hurried around the front of the car and folded himself into the seat. Corralling Jess was going to be every bit as hard as he expected. "So what can you tell me about this Hammy?"

"I don't know about now, but ten or twelve years ago, he was trouble. Both him and his older brother. Theft, drugs, you name it. He's the last person I would have imagined Priscilla with."

"Maybe he's changed in the last eight years."

"Or Priscilla changed."

About five miles outside of town, she pulled beneath a wrought iron arch. Letters spelling out Driggers had been worked into the intricate design. A hedge-lined driveway snaked through a sprawling front yard to loop around a three-tiered fountain. Beyond that lay a house that could accommodate half the population of Harmony Grove. It stretched across the landscape, opulent and majestic with tall, arched windows, multiple alcoves and gables, two chimneys and a porch flanked by marble columns that soared the full two stories.

Shane let out a low whistle. "I take it Hammy's not a gas-station attendant."

"He's not. But I'm afraid Hammy can't take the credit. This is the legacy of Carlton Driggers. He started Driggers Porcelain and Pottery forty years ago and built it into an international business. It's just past here, right next door, actually. The old man died a year ago, so everything belongs to Hammy and his brother, Spike, now."

When they rang the bell, one side of the double door swung inward to reveal an older man in a dark suit, the epitome of the starchy English butler. "May I help you?"

Jess stepped forward. "Is Hammy here?"

"Who may I tell him is calling?"

"Jess Parker. I'm Priscilla's sister."

He invited them into the foyer and excused himself with a nod that was more of a half bow. In less than a minute, he was back. "Come with me."

He led them though the house, then pushed open a set of wooden double doors. The room looked like a den, with bookcases lining two walls and a lavish entertainment center built into a third. A leather sectional wrapped a square piece of thick beveled glass held up by two porcelain black panthers.

Hammy occupied one end of the sectional. He obviously wasn't expecting guests. And he obviously didn't care that he *looked* as if he wasn't expecting guests. He sat slouched, legs sprawled in front of him, his hair mussed. He hadn't bothered to don a shirt, either. In fact, he probably hadn't moved from his spot on the couch for some time. An open bag of chips sat on the coffee table, along with a partially eaten sandwich and two bottles of scotch, one half-empty, the other completely drained. There wasn't a glass in sight.

Jess approached the motionless form on the couch. "Hammy?"

For several moments, Hammy didn't acknowledge their presence. His glazed eyes rested on the big-screen TV at the other end of the room. Some kind of action flick was playing. Thriller, sci-fi, spy movie, Shane wasn't sure. Hammy probably wasn't, either. Though his gaze was fixed there, his attention appeared to be elsewhere. Finally, he dragged his eyes from the television and nodded toward the other end of the sofa.

Jess settled onto the couch, leaving room for Shane to sit at the end. "This is my friend Shane." She drew in a deep breath. "Thanks for seeing us. I know things aren't good for you right now." When he didn't respond, she continued. "This is so unlike Priscilla. I was hoping you might be able to help me understand why she did it."

"I don't know why she did it." The words were slurred. The man was drunk, which wasn't any big surprise.

"Did she seem depressed at all?"

He shook his head. "I never saw Prissy depressed about anything."

"She didn't seem upset or worried?"

"Not that I could tell."

"Do you know if she was involved in anything… illegal? Was there maybe something she had that someone might want?"

His eyes met Jess's, and concern flashed in their watery depths. "What do you mean?"

"Someone ransacked her house. They took the hard drive out of her computer. Any idea what they would be looking for?"

His gaze fluttered away to settle on the television, and he ran a hand over his stubble. "No idea."

Shane mentally ticked off the two telltale signs of lying. Hammy knew something. Now if Jess could just loosen his tongue. The scotch should help.

"I was told she OD'd on oxycodone. Did she do drugs?"

"Yeah, some. Nothing hard. Mostly weed."

"How about oxycodone?"

"Once or twice." He leaned forward to grasp the scotch around the neck of the bottle and brought it to his mouth. Several drops dribbled down his chest. Just what Shane suspected. Hammy was measuring his drinks by the bottle rather than the glass.

"Can you think of anyone who would want to see her dead?"

He looked at her sharply. "She killed herself. What are you talking about?"

"We're not so sure. There are things that make us think she might have been murdered."

Shane cringed. The woman didn't know the meaning of the word *covert*. But he didn't have time to concern himself with her boldness. Hammy sprang to his feet, then staggered sideways until he found his balance. "That stupid, opportunistic woman! Why couldn't she keep her mouth shut?"

Except for a soft intake of air and a brief widening of her eyes, Jess didn't react. He was impressed. Maybe she was better at this than he thought.

"What do you mean?" she asked, her tone level. "What did she do?"

Hammy set the bottle back on the table and sank onto the couch, once again in control. Even drunk, he knew he had said too much. "I don't know. That's just how she was. She talked too much and probably ticked off the wrong person."

Shane studied him. Realizing his slip sobered him up better than a cold shower and a strong cup of coffee. But Jess persisted. "How is that opportunistic?"

"I don't know. She took advantage of every situation. No matter what happened, she came out on top. You never wanted to argue with her. No way you'd ever win."

Jess nodded. "I figured that out a long time ago." She pulled a receipt from her purse and scrawled something on the back. "Here's my cell number. If you think of anything that might help me figure out what happened, give me a call."

He took the paper and, without looking at it, laid

it on the table. That phone call wasn't likely to happen. Whatever Hammy knew, he wasn't going to share it with Jess.

She stood to leave. "Thanks for talking to us. We'll let ourselves out."

Shane followed her across the room, and when she pushed open the double doors and stepped through, she almost bumped into an older, more hardened version of Hammy.

"What are you doing here?" He stared down at her, coal-black eyes reflecting the suspicion in his tone.

Jess didn't flinch. "Hello, Spike. Just offering my condolences. I lost my sister, but he lost his girlfriend."

Spike studied her in silence, his gaze as hard as flint. Shane resisted the urge to drape a protective arm across her shoulder. It wasn't necessary. She was holding her own. Finally, Spike brushed past them and into the room where Hammy sat.

Shane waited until they were outside to question Jess. "What was that all about? Bad blood between you two?"

"There never was before. I don't think he wants me talking to Hammy."

"I'd venture that's a good guess. You think he knows something?"

She climbed into the driver's seat, and he slid in opposite her. "Without a doubt."

"What about Hammy?"

"I still can't imagine Prissy with him. She was always so goody-goody. But like Hammy said, she was also opportunistic. So she had probably figured out how to look past his faults to the dollar signs beneath."

She cranked the car and began moving around the loop, the fountain to her left. It was lit now, each tier flowing into the next in shimmering gold cascades. She glanced over at him. "Do you think he had anything to do with her death?"

"No." Hammy wasn't exactly an upstanding citizen. Ten minutes in the same room with him told him that. The man probably had a rap sheet long enough to stretch from Harmony Grove to Lakeland. But he didn't kill Priscilla.

She eased to a stop under the wrought iron arch. "He insists he has no idea who could have wanted her dead."

Yeah, that was what he said. He also wouldn't look them in the eye when he said it. "Do you believe him?"

"Not for a second."

FIVE

The slightest hint of dawn sifted through the gaps in the miniblinds. Jessica straightened her legs, then stopped midroll at a familiar warm pressure in the center of her back. Buttons.

Four days ago, she had no intention of allowing a dog in her bed. But when she trudged to the master bedroom Buttons's first night home, he gazed up at her with such pathetic longing, all her objections dissolved. He had no one, not a soul in the world. She had been there. She could relate.

Now she had friends, at least close acquaintances, and other students at the dojo. But that long-ago night when she fled Harmony Grove, she'd been totally alone. She hitched a ride to Miami and spent four weeks in a shelter before landing a job and saving enough to make it on her own.

She wiggled onto her other side and ran a hand down Buttons's back. His tail thumped against the mattress, and he opened one eye. He had settled in well. The quivering had stopped almost immediately. And devotion was replacing the insecurity in his eyes. Someday he would have to go. Just not yet.

Jessica rolled from the bed and put Buttons on the floor. She had an investigation to do. And she wanted to get away before Shane showed up.

It wasn't that she didn't like him. Because she did. The attraction was there right from the start, at least on her end. She had always found guys like him irresistible—the quick wit, hair a little too long, air a little too careless—those free spirits that can't be nailed down.

But that was where the resemblance to the other men in her life ended. Beneath that carefree exterior was a compassionate heart. She had given him a glimpse into her childhood, and the sympathy he'd shown caught her off guard. She wasn't used to that kind of concern from guys who possessed his combination of charm and good looks. She had been almost tempted to drop her defenses. And that couldn't be a good thing.

She pulled her keys from her purse and put the strap over her shoulder. Now to find out what Prissy had gotten mixed up in. Hammy was somehow involved. She was sure of it. Or he at least knew something. He just wasn't talking, even half-drunk.

And Spike…well, he had bumped Buck out of first place on her list of suspects. The way he stared her down in the wide hall—she hadn't missed the overt threat. It was there in his gaze, so strong it was almost palpable.

She stepped out the front door and cast a glance at Yesteryear Antiques. Shane's car still sat in the small parking lot on the side. Unless he was watching her through one of the upstairs windows, he wouldn't see her leave.

Her main fault with him was that he didn't take her concerns seriously. Or maybe he did and didn't want her to get involved. Either way, he was wasting his breath. She was seeking justice for Prissy, with or without Shane's support.

Her first task would be getting the police report. Maybe even the autopsy report, if it was available. Early on a Saturday morning, Chief Branch wasn't likely to be at the station. She would get a lot further with Alan or Tommy.

She had just unlocked her car door when her phone started to ring. Instead of a number, the word *unavailable* stretched across the small display. She slid into the seat and put the phone to her ear.

"Jessica." It was just her name, but the coarse whisper made it sound like a threat.

Dread trickled over her, raising the fine hairs on the back of her neck. "Who is this?"

"Leave Harmony Grove now. If you don't, bad things will happen."

The line clicked dead.

She stared at the screen, but it didn't hold any answers. Only a handful of people in Harmony Grove had her cell phone number. Shane was one. So was

BethAnn. And she had given her number to Lexi. None of them would make a call like that.

Then there was Hammy. From the little contact she had had with him last night, he wasn't much more likely than the others. But he had tossed the number on the coffee table, and Spike had gone into the room as she was leaving. Judging from that brief encounter in the hallway, she was pretty sure where the call came from. Well, Spike could make all the threats he wanted to. She wasn't leaving until she had answers.

When she arrived at the tan stucco building downtown, she breathed a sigh of relief. A Harmony Grove police cruiser sat in the parking lot. But it didn't belong to Branch. His had Chief prominently displayed on the side. He drove it everywhere, whether he was on duty or not. He was proud of his position and reminded the residents of Harmony Grove of it as often as he could. If not with the car, then with the uniform and conceited swagger that he always carried with it.

She parked next to a royal blue 1968 Mustang, which she guessed belonged to Alan, and hurried inside. She was right. Alan sat at the desk, bent over a report, pen in hand. He looked up when she entered and flashed her a friendly smile.

"You're here bright and early. What's up?"

She took a seat opposite his desk. "I'd like to see whatever you have on Prissy's death."

"Sure." He rolled his chair across the vinyl-tile

floor and opened a file drawer without getting up. "I don't know if this will give you what you're looking for. It was a pretty open and shut case." He rolled back to the desk, turned the folder so she could view it right side up and flipped back the cover.

In the front was an envelope holding about a dozen photos. She removed the stack and began to thumb through them. The first several were pictures of Prissy lying in bed. Although her eyes were closed, she didn't look peaceful. Maybe it was the way her head lay rotated to the side, or the way the sheets and comforter were twisted around her. Maybe it was just knowing she was dead. It all seemed surreal.

The next photo showed Priscilla's nightstand. Next to the lamp sat a white ceramic mortar and pestle. Did she crush the oxycodone? Why not just swallow the pills? The answer came almost immediately. A close-up of Priscilla's hip revealed a syringe tucked into one of the folds of the bed sheets.

Jessica laid the photo down, suddenly feeling cold and hollow inside. Her gaze met Alan's, and she shook her head. "No."

"Maybe you should skip the pictures."

"The oxycodone was injected?" Her eyes returned to the picture to stare in disbelief. "Prissy wouldn't have done that. She was terrified of needles. She never would have injected something she could have swallowed."

"Maybe she outgrew her fear of needles."

Maybe. But enough to inject something when she had a choice? Not likely. It was just one more piece of a very ugly puzzle.

She moved the picture to the back of the stack. The final two were shots of the room. Nothing out of the ordinary. The closet door was open, and a pair of jeans hung over the back of the desk chair with a blouse draped on top. Other than that, nothing appeared out of place. Priscilla had grown up to be as neat as she'd been when Jessica left. Always the perfect little princess. Except it was looking as if she had somehow managed to get herself killed.

Jessica slid the photos back into the envelope and removed two stapled pages from the folder. It was the police report. They responded to a call from Edith DelRoss that Priscilla hadn't shown up for work and wasn't answering her phone. Branch and Tommy Patterson arrived to find no sign of forced entry. All doors and windows were locked.

She stopped reading for several moments. Whoever injected the oxycodone, they must have come in the slider, or else Priscilla had gotten up and let them in.

Or they'd used a key.

Fear slid down her throat and settled in her gut. She had been sleeping in that house all week, confident that no one could get in since she had secured the sliders her first day there. As soon as she left the police station, she would stop by the hardware store. She would have the locks changed before nightfall.

She returned her eyes to the report. The rest confirmed what she had learned in the photos. Priscilla was found lying in bed on her back, dressed in her two-piece flannel pajamas. The initial report listed the cause of death as apparent drug overdose, possible suicide. The prints lifted from the mortar, pestle and syringe were later determined to be Priscilla's, and when the toxicology report came back, Branch prepared a supplement. Her death was definitively ruled a suicide.

At the back of the file was an autopsy report. She skimmed through stats like height, weight, eye and hair color. The clothing section agreed with what she already knew. When she reached the words *External Examination,* she began to read more carefully. Subject was a well-developed, well-nourished white female. No surgical scars. No cuts or lacerations. There was evidence of light bruising on her upper arms and wrists.

Jessica's gaze shot to Alan's face. "Where did the bruises come from?"

Alan leaned forward to read the line she pointed out. "I don't know. Tommy and Chief responded to the call, and Chief did most of the investigation. I wasn't involved."

Jessica nodded. Lexi said Priscilla and Hammy had had a fight the night before she died. Maybe he got a little rough with her.

Or maybe the bruising happened when someone restrained her to administer a lethal injection.

She lowered her eyes to the page and resumed reading. Puncture to underside of lower left arm, one inch from bend of elbow, possible injection site. No other remarkable findings on external examination.

"Can I get copies of all this?"

"Sure."

Alan rose from the chair, file in hand, as the front door swung open. Chief Branch swaggered inside.

"Oh, hi, Chief. I didn't expect you in today."

"I was driving by and thought I'd stop. So what's going on here?"

Jessica tensed. Branch's gaze was leveled on her rather than Alan. He stopped because he saw her car in the parking lot.

Alan answered before she could respond. "I'm copying some things for Jessica."

"What kind of things?"

"Things on her sister—you know, police report, autopsy report."

Branch took the folder from Alan. "You go on. I'll take it from here."

Alan raised a brow in question, but instead of arguing with his chief, he returned to the report he had been working on when she arrived. Branch cocked his head toward the door on the right. Gold stenciled letters read Grady Branch, Chief of Police.

She followed him into the room, and he closed the door behind them.

"So you want copies of Priscilla's file. There are

procedures for that." He dropped the file onto his desk and settled his girth into the oversize executive chair behind it. "You can't march in here and expect us to drop everything to accommodate you. Submit a written request, and we'll see what we can do."

"You can keep your reports. I've already seen what I needed to see." She turned to go, but before she reached the door, his voice stopped her.

"You know, missy, you're doing way too much sticking your nose where it doesn't belong. I already warned you about stirring up trouble. People who don't heed sound advice sometimes get more than they bargained for. Accidents can happen, you know."

She narrowed her gaze and stared him down for several moments. "If you think your threats scare me, you don't know me very well." Then she turned and strode from the room, out the front door and to her car.

Eight years ago, Buck beat her to a pulp and she ran. As a result, Priscilla endured four years of her own private hell. Now Prissy was gone, her life ended, her future brutally taken from her.

This time Jess wasn't running. She was older, wiser and tougher. And dead set determined to right past wrongs.

Priscilla's killer's and her own.

The Bug shuddered to a stop in the driveway, but Jess didn't immediately get out. All morning long, he had periodically checked the window, watching for her to return while trying not to obsess. But she was so determined. And so reckless.

He crossed the street and headed up her driveway. When he reached the car door, she still sat in the driver's seat, phone in hand, scrolling, studying, then scrolling again.

He tapped lightly on the window, trying not to scare her. She started anyway, shoved the phone facedown on her leg and turned startled eyes on him. The next instant, the tension visibly fled her body, and she opened the door.

He smiled down at her. "Hey, you. Did you get a new phone?"

She shook her head and climbed from the car, pulling a plastic Tandy Hardware bag across the seat with her. "No, it's Priscilla's. I decided to pay another visit to Lexi, Priscilla's best friend. The night before Prissy died, she and Prissy went out. Prissy was upset, said she and Hammy had gotten into a fight. She left her phone in Lexi's car."

She swung the door shut and headed toward the house. "Actually, Lexi told me all this the first time. What she didn't mention then was that she didn't find Prissy's phone until this past weekend. So she still had it."

He followed her up the concrete walk. "Anything interesting?"

"She's only got about twenty contacts. I was comparing her recent calls with them when you came up. So far, all the numbers match the ones labeled Pappy's, Hammy Cell, Lexi Cell or Lexi Home."

"What about pictures?" Maybe whoever ransacked the Parker house was after something on Priscilla's phone.

"I haven't looked at those yet." She unlocked the door and motioned him inside. "I did go by the police station, though. Alan was there, so I got to look at the police and autopsy reports before Branch arrived and threw me out."

Shane cocked a brow at her. "He threw you out?"

"Not really threw me out. Just basically told me that if I didn't stop snooping, I was going to meet with an unfortunate accident."

Shane clenched his fists. Branch wasn't just conceited, overbearing and condescending. He was a bully. And he was dirty. Maybe he didn't kill Priscilla Parker. But he was probably covering for someone who did. And if Jess didn't back off, she was going to be the next target. The thought sent panic spiraling through him.

He drew in a deep breath and tried to distance himself from the situation. He would do everything he could to protect her. It was his job. But he was making it personal. And that was never a good thing.

He settled onto the couch next to her, reining in the last of his wayward emotions. "So did you learn anything?"

"Actually I did. The oxycodone that Prissy overdosed on was injected. There was a mortar and pestle on her nightstand, and a syringe in the bed beside her, all covered with her prints." She crossed her arms and settled back into the cushions. As usual, Buttons had plastered himself to her opposite hip. "There's only one problem. Prissy was terrified of needles. She would never have injected herself when swallowing the pills would accomplish the same thing."

"She was terrified of needles as a child. You don't know about as an adult."

Jess rose from the couch and began to pace. "There was also slight bruising on her upper arms and wrists, as if someone might have held her down."

"That could be from anything. If she was really as terrified of needles as you say, she would have fought like a wildcat. She'd have bruises on her legs, too."

"Maybe someone sat across her legs to pin her down. Whoever did it, I'm sure he had help." She stopped pacing and planted both hands on her hips. "You can't deny that the whole thing is suspicious. Priscilla wasn't an intravenous drug user. There were no other needle marks anywhere on her. Just the one on her left arm, right below—" She stopped midsentence, her eyes wide.

"What is it?" he asked.

"The needle mark was on her left arm."

He stared up at her, waiting for her to continue. He didn't see the significance. "Yes?"

"Priscilla was left-handed. There's no indication she had ever injected anything before. But let's assume this one time she did. Do you really think she'd use her non-dominant hand?"

"You have a point."

She studied him for several moments, brows raised. "You're not going to come up with some way to explain it away?"

"There are too many things that don't add up." He may as well level with her. He wasn't going to talk her out of getting involved. He had already tried. His best course of action was to work with her. She said she preferred to work alone, but that would probably change once she knew who he was. Maybe after her background check came back. He didn't want any surprises. "Hammy knows something, and I'd bet Branch does, too."

"I don't think either of them killed her." She sank back onto the couch next to him.

"I agree. But since there was no sign of forced entry, someone must have had a key."

"Or they knew there was a key under the flower pot in the front and used it to come in."

"There was a key under the flower pot?"

"Eight years ago, yes, except for when Prissy would hide it and lock me out. It wasn't there when

I arrived a few days ago, but maybe that's because someone took it."

"Uh-huh." He thought for a moment. "And don't forget about Buttons."

Her eyes widened. "You're right. Buttons knew the killer. Otherwise, he wouldn't have let him into the house."

"True. And we know she had something they were looking for, something incriminating."

She nodded. "A recording maybe? A document? A photo?"

"Which brings us back to the phone." He reached in front of her to pick up the item from the end table. "What do you say we look at these pictures?"

"Sounds good."

She leaned closer to better see the display, pressing her shoulder against his. As he touched the menu icon and brought up the photos, a clean, fresh scent surrounded him. It was less assuming than perfume, more like body wash or shampoo. An unexpected longing filled his chest, something he had kept at bay for three years.

He drew in a deep breath and pulled his mind back to the task at hand. He would be more likely to notice subtle clues if he focused on what he was doing instead of Jess.

He scrolled through photo after photo, each of them unremarkable, then stopped. Three men stood in a semicircle. A fourth barely made it into the picture, with only a potbelly and chin visible at the right-hand edge.

Jess pointed at the phone. "That's Hammy and Spike."

"What about the third man?"

"I don't recognize him."

"Can you tell where they are?"

She shook her head. "Not with the photo this size."

"Have you got a USB cable and a computer you can view it on?"

"No on the USB cable. And the computer is minus a hard drive."

"I've got both. How about bringing it over to my place." He would save the photo and have Ross try to get an ID on the third man. With nothing more than a belly and chin, ID'ing the fourth was probably impossible.

"That sounds good. Then I need to get back and get ready for Prissy's funeral." She rose from the couch and cast a glance at the Tandy Hardware bag sitting on the end table. "I also need to change the locks."

"That's not a bad idea." He should have suggested it himself, just in case.

"The day they found Prissy, they had to break in. Everything was locked up tight. So either she let the killers in, they pried the sliders the same way I did, or they had a key."

He frowned. "I'll be glad to change them for you."

She swung open the front door and smiled back at him. "Thanks, but I've got it."

He wasn't surprised. She had *independent* written all over her. He pulled the door shut behind him. She had already twisted the lock.

"What do you say we do that movie tonight? I'll even treat you to Pappy's first."

She cocked a brow and flashed him a quirky grin. "Are you asking me out on a date?"

"Just a friendly dinner. Nothing your boyfriend back home would object to."

She responded with a sarcastic snort. "I dumped the boyfriend eight months ago. You know that crooked business partner I was telling you about?"

"Yeah?"

"One and the same."

"Ouch." The creep hit her personal and her professional life all in one blow.

"He's not the first lowlife I've had the misfortune of knowing. That's why I'm still single. And I fully intend to stay that way."

"Me, too." For an entirely different reason. He didn't have a string of bad relationships that soured him on love. There was just one—a match as near perfect as could be. He thought it would last forever. But he made an arrest, a vengeful brother took action and a lifetime of happiness was shattered in a single moment.

He stepped onto the curb, and his gaze followed the sidewalk to the redbrick building topped by a white steeple. He nodded toward the inviting facade. "What do you think of Cornerstone Community Church down there?"

She shrugged. "Don't know. Never been."

"I'm thinking of trying it out tomorrow. I was hoping I wouldn't have to go alone."

"Pappy's I'll do. When it comes to church, you're on your own."

He cocked a brow at her. "You sound pretty adamant."

"Let's just say God and I don't have a whole lot to do with each other."

"That's a shame." He started up the steps with a sense of heaviness in his chest. She hadn't just closed herself off from people. She had shut God out of her life, too.

He pulled the key from his pocket and let them into his apartment. Across the room, the steeple of the church sat framed in the window, its cross promising hope and healing. If only he could introduce Jess to the God he knew.

But that wasn't likely to happen. They weren't going to be together long enough for him to have any kind of impact on her life. Once Priscilla's killers were found and brought to justice, she would head back to Miami. And when his case was solved, the Bureau would send him somewhere else.

That now familiar longing stabbed through him, tinged with regret.

And for the first time in three years, he wished things could be different.

SIX

Jessica strolled down the sidewalk, purse slung over one shoulder and a plastic bag containing lunch swinging at her other side. BethAnn's was only a quarter mile from home. So she had left her Bug in the driveway, snuggled in next to Prissy's Lotus. She may as well conserve the gas. And the weather was perfect for walking. The cold snap had passed, and daytime temperatures had once again returned to their typical mid-to high seventies.

Yesterday she had driven home at lunchtime to grab a sandwich and take Buttons out. Today she didn't even have to do that. Shane had seen her hurrying around in the middle of the day and offered to come over and walk Buttons so she wouldn't have to leave work. The next thing she knew, she was giving him a key.

And ever since, she had alternated between trying to convince herself she hadn't made a big mistake and suspecting she had lost her mind. She had known him for only one week. But there was something about him that inspired trust. He had a frankness and honesty that was reassuring. Maybe there was one man on the planet who wasn't out to use her.

At the least, he was intriguing. He was a commitment-phobic roamer, happy, carefree and without roots. But he had a serious side, too, the part of him that empathized with her and somehow connected with her pain.

And he went to church. He even had a Bible sitting on his coffee table. And it wasn't covered in dust. He actually read it, as evidenced by the worn leather cover and the dog-eared pages.

But in the one way that mattered, he was just like the other men in her life, starting with three fathers and ending with a short string of boyfriends—one morning she would get up and he would be gone.

With a sigh, she reached into the back pocket of her dress jeans and pulled out a key. Yesterday was her first day at BethAnn's. Everyone who stopped by had already spoken to her at Prissy's funeral. So the raised eyebrows at seeing her back in Harmony Grove and condolences for her loss had already been dispensed with before the start of her workweek. And there hadn't been a single reference to her past at either the funeral or BethAnn's. Maybe everyone was content to leave it where it belonged—in the past.

BethAnn had spent the day teaching her how to cut fabric, stock and straighten shelves and use the cash register and credit card machine. She had even entrusted her with keys. This morning she would get the crash course. BethAnn had a doctor's appointment and would be more than an hour late.

She let herself into the store and headed for the back where a large room housed a refrigerator, sink and small cabinet. A long wooden table sat in the center, surrounded by chairs. This was where BethAnn offered her craft classes. When she went on maternity leave, the classes would stop. Jessica had never been crafty enough herself to teach anyone else.

Midway to the refrigerator, she froze. Shards of glass littered the vinyl-tile floor next to the fridge, and several slats in the blinds were cocked at odd angles. Goose bumps cascaded over her, and she swiveled her head to cast an uneasy glance behind her. With a single index finger, she swung the blinds away from the window. The lower pane had been raised, covering a fist-size hole in the upper pane. She backed away, heart pounding. Someone had broken into the store.

She called the police, then walked up and down the aisles, checking the shelves. Nothing looked touched, no product obviously missing. The intruder evidently wasn't interested in items to pawn. Maybe he was looking for cash. But the drawers and safe would wait. After watching Alan at work, she knew better than to risk destroying prints.

When a large uniformed figure filled the doorway, her heart fell. Not Branch again. Since she had come back, he had responded to every call she made. It was as if he was waiting, poised and ready.

"So what seems to be the problem?"

"The store was broken into last night. I came in this morning and found a shattered window in the back."

He stared down at her with that blend of condescension and disdain that he had mastered so well. "Have you noticed how trouble just seems to follow you?"

"Only here in Harmony Grove. I'd say someone's trying to run me off. Why don't you tell them something for me—they're wasting their time."

His puffy lips turned upward in an irreverent smirk, and he pulled a spiral-bound pad from his shirt pocket. "Show me this broken window."

She led him to the back and watched as he attempted to lift prints from the glass and surrounding wall. In spite of his rudeness on first arriving, he seemed to be taking extra care with dusting on the fine black powder, transferring what he found to tape and identifying the location of each print. His attention was likely for BethAnn's sake, not her own.

"It looks as if I got some good prints. They may belong to BethAnn, but we'll see." He walked back into the main part of the store. "Does anything seem to be missing?"

"Not that I've discovered. BethAnn doesn't leave

cash in the drawer overnight, and I haven't noticed anything missing from the shelves."

He nodded and walked toward the counter near the front of the store. A cash register and credit card machine sat on top, and four long drawers occupied the space below. Branch pulled open the top drawer with one latex-clad finger, and she leaned forward to look inside.

Her eyes widened, and she gasped. Someone had rifled through the receipts. Before she left last night, she had put them in a neat stack and paper-clipped them together. They were still paper-clipped, but none of the sides lined up anymore and several of the corners were dog-eared.

"I don't know if any are missing, but the receipts have been gone through."

"Any idea why?"

She shook her head. As far as financial information, only the name and last four digits of the credit card number appeared. "There's not enough there for anyone to really use."

The other two drawers appeared undisturbed. The middle one contained extra staples, register tape and other office supplies. The bottom held plastic bags and miscellaneous items.

While Branch dusted the top drawer for prints, she wandered around, taking a closer look at the items on the shelves. A small housewares section with candle holders, vases and knickknacks occupied the front of the store. She moved slowly down the aisle, eyes roving over each object, then hesitated. Yesterday afternoon, she had unpacked a case of figurines and arranged them in three neat rows of four each. One row now contained three.

But that wasn't what drew her attention. The missing figurine may have been sold the prior afternoon. But the remaining ones seemed to have been moved from their original positions. The rows were no longer ruler-straight, and some of the figurines had been turned several degrees. A shopper may have picked up one or two, but not all of them.

She looked over at Chief Branch, who appeared to be just finishing his work on the drawer. "This is going to sound crazy, but all of these figurines have been disturbed. And one's missing."

Branch made his way over to where she stood. "You're sure?"

"I'm positive. I unpacked and put every one of them on the shelf myself."

Branch nodded. "I'll go ahead and dust those, too."

After a thorough inspection of the store, she returned to find him brushing fine black powder over a good portion of the counter.

"I decided to get this area, too, just in case."

She studied him, brows drawn together. Branch didn't take anything this seriously. Even for Beth-Ann. What was he up to? His actions raised as many questions as the break-in itself.

BethAnn entered moments after he left. "Branch

was headed out of the parking lot as I was pulling in. I take it he didn't come looking for embroidery or candle-making supplies."

Jessica laughed in spite of herself. "As entertaining as it is to picture Branch getting in touch with his feminine side, that wasn't why he was here. I arrived this morning to find a window broken."

Alarm filled BethAnn's eyes. "Was anything taken?"

"Not that I can tell. Yesterday's receipts have been disturbed, and the Driggers figurines I put up seem to have been moved." She closed the drawer that had been left open by Branch. "By the way, did one of the figurines sell?"

"Yes, right at the end of the day."

She nodded slowly. So everything was accounted for. Apparently, they were dealing with a burglar who broke in to look at receipts and play with figurines.

And Chief Branch eagerly dusted everything as if he were trying to solve a murder investigation.

It made no sense. None at all.

Shane sat at his desk watching page after page spill from the printer, phone pressed against his left ear. Spike's criminal report was surprisingly short. Maybe he wasn't the renegade that Shane initially thought. Or maybe he was just smart enough to not get caught. Hammy obviously wasn't. Twenty pages lay in the tray, and the printer didn't show any signs of stopping.

"These should be your guys," Ross said. "Carlton Driggers had only two sons."

Shane pulled the stack from the printer and laid it beside the much smaller one already on the desk. "Yep, this is them." The photos left no doubt. Wilford and Thaddeus. No wonder they chose nicknames.

"Wilford has managed to stay clean the past few years. Maybe he's turned over a new leaf, figured his younger brother was getting into enough trouble for both of them."

Shane snickered. "I doubt that. I think he's just gotten smarter. Or luckier."

"Any easy way to get inside their business?"

"Sometimes these factories do tours." If so, he might have an opportunity to slip away from the group and do some snooping.

"What are your chances of getting a job there?"

"Probably not good, unless the hiring decisions are made by someone other than the Driggers brothers. When I went with Jess to pay Hammy a visit, big brother didn't look too happy to see us."

"Well, go ahead and give it a try."

"Will do. I don't know anything about making porcelain. But I could try to get something in shipping and receiving. I'm more than qualified to handle boxes." And the Bureau would take care of the winning resume. "What about the Lotus? Anything back on it yet?"

"Yeah. It's a 2011 Lotus Exige, registered to Priscilla Parker. But it was bought with a cashier's check drawn on the account of Thaddeus Driggers."

"That's what I've heard around town, that Hammy bought it for her. Pretty lavish gift for a girlfriend."

"Yeah, to the tune of eighty-two grand and some change."

Once Ross ended the call, Shane took the time to read the two new reports more thoroughly. Spike's was all of three pages. After three possession charges and two burglary charges, he seemed to have learned his lesson. His last arrest was over six years ago.

Hammy hadn't figured it out yet. He spent more time *in* jail than out. In fact, he was currently free on bond awaiting trial on his latest charge, possession with intent to sell. As with several of the other charges, the arresting agency was Lakeland P.D. Hammy hadn't gotten into trouble in Harmony Grove in over five years. Maybe he didn't think he would get away with it in his own hometown.

Or maybe someone in Harmony Grove was covering for him.

He pulled a folder that he had previously labeled Background Checks from the desk drawer. Two others had come in the prior day. He flipped the folder open, and a printed black-and-white photo of Jessica stared back at him. She had had only one arrest as an adult, down in Miami, a few months after her eighteenth birthday. Apparently she helped hold up a convenience store by driving the getaway car.

She had told him about getting in trouble as a teen, said it was stupid stuff. She was right. And judging from the photos, getting hauled in didn't shake her in the slightest. Her eyes shone with rebellion, and the lift of her chin radiated stubborn pride, as if each picture was snapped just after a defiant toss of her head.

The latest photo, though, held none of that. Her dark eyes were wide and infused with fear. It was as if she had just realized she was an adult, and all the ramifications that went with it. Justice looked a little scarier from the other side of that all-important birthday. Life wasn't a game anymore.

At least she made a wise choice. She took a plea bargain and agreed to testify against the two guys in exchange for her charges being dropped.

Shane laid the two newest reports on top and closed the file. Under Jess's lay another one. The criminal history portion simply said No Record Found. Branch was clean.

He rose from the chair, dropped his keys into his pocket and strode to the door. The past few days he had spent a lot of time hanging out downtown, sitting in the local coffee shop and fast-food places, keeping his eyes and ears open. Tonight he would hit Pappy's Pizzeria again. It was a great spot for people watching. The place was always packed.

When he reached the bottom of the stairs, he headed toward the sidewalk. From his temporary home, all of downtown was within easy walking distance. His route to Pappy's took him right past BethAnn's Fabrics and Crafts, and he couldn't resist a glance through the plate glass window. BethAnn stood at the cash register speaking with a customer, and Jess walked briskly toward one of the aisles carrying three bolts of fabric. He stopped walking to watch her.

She wore a patterned scoop-necked tee paired with those designer jeans and ever-present platform boots that were so much more Jess than last week's skirt and blazer had been. In profile, her hair appeared almost jet black against skin that had lost most of its summertime tan. The dark ends framed her face and curled gently away from her long neck.

That exotic beauty had probably captivated more than one unsuspecting man. But that wouldn't have been her fault. She didn't flirt or use her feminine wiles to get what she wanted. She had the strength and confidence to go after whatever she needed without help from anyone else. And a bluntness that he found refreshing. There was no pretense with Jess.

Once she had the bolts stuffed into their proper slots, she turned to make her way back to the front of the store. Her eyes met his through the window, and a smile climbed up her cheeks. According to the sign on the door, it was almost closing time. Maybe he could convince her to go to Pappy's with him again. It was the best way he knew to keep her out of trouble, at least for a couple of hours. And it helped stave off some of the loneliness.

He swung open the front door and stepped inside. "Hey, you."

BethAnn waved an enthusiastic greeting while Jess met him at the door. "Hey. What are you up to?"

"Getting ready for dinner at Pappy's."

"Again? You're not tired of pizza yet?"

"Pappy's has more than pizza. But I was hoping a certain neighbor of mine would be willing to keep me company."

Before she had an opportunity to respond, the bell on the door sounded, and an older woman marched in wearing one of those big hairdos from the 1960s. Her eager eyes roved the store then settled on him.

"I've seen you around but haven't had a chance to properly introduce myself." She stuck out her hand. "Carolyn Platt."

"Shane Dalton."

"Are you Jessica's boyfriend? I noticed you two arrived around the same time."

He cast a glance at Jessica, who grinned back at him. "I'm afraid that was purely coincidental. We never met till the night she arrived."

"I see. Well, welcome to Harmony Grove." She turned those eager eyes on Jess. "You heard what happened to the Tandys, right?"

"No. What happened to the Tandys?" Jessica's tone was flat, as if she had had to answer one too many knock-knock jokes.

"Someone broke into their house last night. Roger got up, and the guy was there. He had a gun, hit Roger upside the head with it. Scared Marge to death, it did. She heard the commotion and got up to find the window open and Roger on the floor unconscious. He has a concussion, went to the hospital and everything. He's back home now."

"That's awful," BethAnn said. She had made her way over to where they stood the moment Carolyn began her story. "Do they have any idea who it was?"

"Not a clue. Roger said the guy had on one of those knit things that covers the face, except for eye holes and an opening for the mouth."

Jess seemed to have grown a shade paler. "Was anything taken?"

"Not that they could tell. My guess is if Roger hadn't gotten up when he did, the guy might have robbed them blind."

"Pretty scary." BethAnn shook her head. "We had a break-in at the store last night, too. They didn't get anything here, either."

Carolyn's eyes widened. "Oh, my. I didn't know

about the store being broken into. Well, I'm not going to keep you. I know it's quitting time."

As soon as the door closed, Jess gave him a crooked grin. "So you got to experience Carolyn Platt, Harmony Grove's most notorious gossip."

"Yeah. It looks as if her only reason for coming in was to fill us in on the latest."

"You got it," BethAnn answered. "The only thing Carolyn enjoys more than being the first to know is being the first to tell." She flipped off a bank of light switches and pulled a set of keys from her purse. "6:05. Time to hit the road."

Shane pushed open the front door and turned to Jess. "You never answered my question."

"I don't believe you asked one."

"Well, I sort of asked you to dinner."

She shook her head. "I can't."

"Come on. It's my treat."

"I can't keep letting you buy me dinner."

She stalked toward the sidewalk, then made a left, heading toward home. He had to hurry to catch up. "Why not?"

"Because I pay my own way. And since I've got to make my sister's house payment next week and hope to have enough left over for groceries, that's out of the question. So I'll eat at home."

"I'm tired of eating alone. Believe me, the cost of your dinner at Pappy's is a small price to pay for your company."

"I feel like a charity case."

"You're not. You're doing me a favor."

She gave him a quirky smile. "Well, in that case…"

"Great."

He put an arm across her shoulder to steer her in the other direction. For Jess, money was tight, no doubt. But getting to know her had pretty well stamped out any thoughts of her benefiting from her sister's death. She was too independent, too set on making her own way. She had some stains on her record, but his gut told him she wasn't any more involved in the shady side of Harmony Grove than he was. And his gut was usually right.

Ten minutes later, they were seated at Pappy's, two iced teas in front of them and salad and pasta dishes ordered.

He smiled across the table at her. "See, isn't this a lot better than dinner alone?"

One corner of her mouth quirked up. "Yeah, you're pretty good company. But I'm used to eating alone. Sometimes it beats the alternative."

"You're awfully jaded."

"Yeah, I probably am. But I have good reason to be."

"You want to talk about it?"

She responded with a snort. "Which one do you want to hear about first, the one who ran my business into the ground or the one who set me up for some hefty jail time? And there were a couple of doozies in between. So dinner alone isn't so bad."

Her tone lacked the bitterness he would have

expected. Instead, it held an odd sort of resignation. She had mastered the art of accepting the past, no matter how ugly, and moving forward with her life. He might be able to learn a thing or two from her.

She took a long swig of her tea. "What about you? Why are you still single?"

He shrugged. "I'm a loner, move around a lot."

She studied him so intently, he had to look away. He wasn't fooling her. She recognized the flippant answer for what it was—a way to avoid the truth. Thinking about telling her he worked for the Bureau was one thing. Drawing back the carefree facade to reveal the tortured man beneath was entirely another. And he wasn't going to go there.

He met her eyes again. "What do you think happened at the Tandys'?"

Two vertical creases formed between her eyebrows. "I don't know what to think. Things like that don't happen in Harmony Grove." She leaned toward him and dropped her voice. "Of course, neither does murder."

"Do you think it's all related?"

"I don't see how. I'm sure Prissy's death and her house being ransacked are related. But I don't see what BethAnn has to do with any of that. Or the Tandys."

"What does Roger Tandy do?"

"He owns Tandy Hardware."

"What about his wife?"

"Marge is a painter."

"Like an artist?"

"Yeah, she does oil paintings."

He nodded slowly. He didn't see a connection, either. "Any chance the Tandys could be mixed up in whatever your sister was?"

"No way. They've always been good Christian people. He even teaches Sunday school at Cornerstone. At least he used to. I can't imagine either of them involved in anything shady."

Maybe they weren't involved—or knowingly, at any rate. But something told him there was a connection between all the seemingly unrelated incidents. He just had to find it.

He prayed that would happen before anyone else got hurt.

SEVEN

Jessica stepped out the front door into the early-morning sunshine, her gaze drifting toward Yesteryear Antiques. She was doing that a lot, subconsciously searching out Shane before she even realized what she was doing. Of course, he was occupying a lot of her conscious thoughts, too.

She had felt that pull of attraction from almost the first moment she saw him. That alone should have been warning enough to steer clear of him. But he was hard to avoid. For one, he lived right across the street. Even if he wasn't dropping by every chance he got, she would still be bumping into him on a regular basis. Next, he was so…friendly. He took the meaning of *neighborly* to new heights, helping her clean up the house, taking her to dinner, sticking up for her against Branch. And third, she had a murder to solve. And like he said, two heads were better than one.

So she was spending way more time with him than she should. But she was a big girl. She could handle it. *He* seemed to be dealing with their closeness just fine. He said he wasn't interested in relationships. Said he was a loner, moved around a lot.

She didn't believe it. Whatever his reason for avoiding emotional entanglements, it had nothing to do with moving around. In fact, it was probably just the opposite—his not staying in one place for long helped him avoid serious relationships. He was running from something. But she would probably never know what. He wasn't exactly Mr. Transparent.

She sighed, chewing on her lower lip. For all she knew, he could be a fugitive. It wouldn't be the first mistake she had made in judging a man's character. And it probably wouldn't be the last.

She rounded the front of her Bug to slip between the two cars sitting side by side in the driveway. Hers hadn't moved in several days, Prissy's even longer. Almost immediately, something caught her eye, white against the tinted driver's side window. A sheet of paper was taped there, folded in half.

She approached the window and pulled the page loose. At least it wasn't a ticket. Even Branch wouldn't be able to find a reason to ticket her in her own driveway.

The paper was lined, with a jagged left-hand edge where it was pulled from a spiral notebook. Block letters filled half the page.

Jessica,
Look under your car. This is a warning. Next

time you won't be so lucky. Quit your snooping and go back to Miami. Remember, accidents can happen.

Her heart began to pound in her chest, sending blood roaring through her ears. What did they do to her car? She dropped to her knees and looked underneath. A six-by-six inch puddle had formed near the inside edge of the front passenger's side tire.

She circled around the car, leaving her purse and lunch on the hood, then knelt next to the right front quarter panel. A steady drip fell from an open tube. Someone had cut her brake line. She pushed herself to her feet, a chill sweeping over her.

Accidents can happen.

Branch had spoken the same words. Would he be bold enough to cut her brake lines and then write something that would instantly draw her thoughts to him? Obviously, he didn't do it himself. He would never get his hands dirty. But did he send someone else?

"Car trouble?"

The deep male voice behind her sent panic shooting through her. The note fluttered to the pavement as she spun and fell back into a fighting stance. Shane stood only four feet in front of her and quickly increased the distance, hands raised.

"Remind me never to sneak up on you."

Relief cascaded over her, and she pressed a hand to her heart. "You startled me."

He grinned. "I noticed. Is something wrong? I was coming down the stairs and saw you looking under your car."

"Something's wrong, all right." She picked up the sheet of paper, grasping a corner between her thumb and index finger. If prints could be lifted from paper, she didn't want to add any more of her own than necessary. "I found this taped to the driver window. Someone cut the brake line."

His green eyes scanned the page she held, and his strong jaw tightened. The quiet fury that passed over his features sent a funny little flutter through her stomach. That wasn't just neighborly concern she saw there.

"This is serious, Jess." Lines of worry had etched themselves into his face.

"I *am* taking it seriously."

"Somehow that's not comforting. My definition of you taking it seriously is getting yourself out of harm's way. Your definition is gearing up for battle."

She planted her hands on her hips. "Well, I'm not running away, if that's what you have in mind. That's exactly what they want me to do."

He heaved an exasperated sigh. "If you refuse to leave, will you at least be careful? Leave some of the investigating to me."

"It's not your responsibility. It's mine."

"I'm making it mine."

He drew in a deep, uneasy breath, eyes scanning

the yards around them. When his gaze returned to her face, the intensity took her aback.

"Can you keep what I'm about to tell you in confidence?" His tone was low, almost conspiratorial.

She nodded, heart pounding in her chest. Whoever Shane was, he wasn't a writer who happened to wander into Harmony Grove looking for a change of scenery.

He dropped his voice even lower. "I'm an agent with the FBI, working undercover on another case. But we think your sister's death might be related."

She nodded again, unable to find her voice. She knew there was more to Shane than he had let on. But she didn't expect this.

"We can help each other out. I have all the resources of the FBI, so I've got access to a lot of information that you don't. But you've got the in with everybody in Harmony Grove. People here will be much more willing to open up to you."

She thought for several moments, lower lip trapped between her teeth. What he said made sense. But there was one problem. "Don't you think it'll be a little suspicious when I have you tag along everywhere? Everyone's going to know you're more than just a concerned neighbor. I don't want to blow your cover."

"It wouldn't be suspicious if everyone thought we were romantically involved. The ruse would be simple to pull off. We just regularly appear in public holding hands, maybe even give them the occasional moonlit kiss in the park." He flashed her a teasing grin. "I recently met someone who would be quite happy to deliver whatever rumor we want to perpetuate to the far reaches of Harmony Grove."

"I think I'm up for it. And Carolyn will make sure everyone gets the juicy details." She tried to mirror his relaxed smile, but it was hard to project a sense of confident ease with the much-too-vivid image of that moonlit kiss stuck in her brain.

"It would all be for show, of course."

"Of course." And she wouldn't allow herself to hope for anything otherwise. She now knew who he was, at least what he did for a living. But there were secrets beneath that carefree exterior that he would probably never share.

She retrieved her purse and lunch from the hood of the car. "I've got to get to work, or I'm going to be late. Walk with me?"

He fell in beside her. "I hope you're not angry with me for not telling you up front. I had to know I could trust you."

Angry? Was he nuts? He trusted her. After a little over a week, he felt confident enough to let her into his world. Warmth spread through her chest, and she squelched a sudden irrational urge to skip down the sidewalk.

She looked up at him, her gaze sincere. "I'm not angry at all. Your trust means a lot to me. I won't let you down."

"Just do me a favor. Try to lay low."

"What do you mean?"

"Don't charge around town asking questions. Try to quietly observe."

She gave him a crooked grin. "Are you saying I'm not stealthy?"

He smiled back at her. "No, I don't think you've mastered stealth yet."

"Okay, I'll try to be less obvious in my quest for the truth."

"Good. So what are you going to do about your car?"

"C.J.'s Garage. I'll call them from work. He'll probably come out and fix it right here. Otherwise, he'll tow it to the shop." And hopefully let her pay for it after she got her first check.

When they reached the store, BethAnn hadn't arrived yet. Jessica unlocked the front door then turned to face Shane. "Well, thanks for seeing me here safely."

"No problem. And I'd like to come back at six to walk you home, if that's okay."

"I'm starting to feel as if I have my own personal bodyguard." Normally it would annoy her. For some reason, it didn't.

"My kind of job." He flashed her a warm smile, one that touched his eyes and made her stomach flip then settle into a quivery lump. "Meanwhile I think I'm going to see if Driggers has any openings."

She raised her brows. "You're going to get a job there?"

"I'm going to try. What better way to keep an eye on Hammy and Spike?"

"Driggers is a pretty big operation, at least for Harmony Grove. I think they run about thirty employees, so you've got a chance."

"Only if Hammy and Spike aren't in charge of hiring."

"Well, good luck." She let the door swing shut and headed toward the back of the store. Going to work for Driggers Porcelain was a great idea. If anyone could pick up secrets there, it would be Shane. He had stealth down to a science.

She slid her sandwich and fruit into the fridge, then grabbed the broom and dustpan from the closet. The store had gotten busy at the end of the prior day. Nothing overwhelming, just steady traffic throughout the afternoon, which kept her from her end-of-the-day task of tidying up.

She worked her way across the front of the store, swinging the broom with long, smooth strokes. When she reached the small housewares section, something shot across the floor and hit the opposite display with a ting. She bent to pick up the object lying there, a piece of porcelain. It had evidently been hidden in the toe space under the bottom shelf.

She turned it over in her hand. It measured about one-fourth by three-fourths of an inch, its glazed surface a rich, deep blue. It didn't come from any of the candle holders, vases or picture frames on the shelf. Maybe the figurines. She held the piece up to one of the smiling country maidens. It perfectly matched the skirt swirling about her calves. Apparently, one of the figurines was broken.

She picked them up one by one, searching for the damaged one. There wasn't a single imperfection, certainly not a quarter-inch wide piece missing out of the skirt. BethAnn said one had sold, but surely the buyer would have noticed that kind of damage.

Maybe the piece hadn't come from any of the twelve figurines. Maybe it had been lying in the bottom of the box when she unpacked it. If she tipped the empty box over when she picked it up, the piece could have fallen out and gotten kicked into the toe space under the shelf.

That was the only explanation she could come up with. But she wasn't convinced. She didn't turn the box over. She was sure of it. And even if she did, if the piece had fallen out and hit the floor, she would have heard something.

So where had that mysterious piece of porcelain come from? It was just one more unanswered question.

And one more piece of a puzzle that seemed to have Driggers at its core.

Shane hoisted a box onto the top of the pallet. His back was beginning to ache in spite of the brace he had been issued.

It was Monday, the start of a new week and a new job. Last Wednesday, he had stopped by Driggers

Porcelain and learned there was a position open in shipping and receiving. He got an interview with the warehouse manager, then went to H.R. to complete the paperwork. Friday afternoon, he got the call telling him to be there Monday morning at seven. Neither Hammy nor Spike had any hand in the entire process.

So here he was, the newest employee of Driggers Porcelain, assigned to the seven to four o'clock shift. It was the perfect opportunity to find out what the Driggers brothers were up to. The only downside was that he had to forego walking Jess to work.

But she wasn't likely to be mugged in broad daylight. At almost 9:00 a.m., downtown was hopping with people opening shops, heading to The Daily Grind for their morning coffee and Danish or just out because they had nothing better to do. So the morning walks were more about spending time with Jess than seeing to her safety.

He hadn't intended for it to happen this way. She was supposed to be nothing more than a connection to the people of Harmony Grove, a way for him to get information from the inside. But over the past two weeks, his perception of her had shifted. She was no longer just the sister of the victim, a valuable contact for his investigation. She had become a friend, a compassionate woman to help ease the loneliness of his solitary existence.

It had been a long time since he had actually connected with someone. It was more than just the forced proximity while they worked together to solve Prissy's murder. Somehow, they connected on a deeper level. Maybe because they were each dealing with their own tragedies. Hers was a series of misfortunes that would leave a lesser person beaten down and defeated. His was one big blow that had knocked his world off its axis. He dealt with his loss by putting up walls that kept anyone from getting too close, all the while praying for strength. She dealt with hers by forging ahead, refusing to let the past get her down, but not allowing herself to trust.

And maybe that was why he felt safe with her. In the eyes of the people of Harmony Grove, they were an item. But he knew the truth—their relationship would never develop beyond friendship. They both had too much baggage.

He checked the last item off the list he had been given and motioned to the forklift driver. The pallet was complete—several cases of vases and figurines ready for shrink-wrapping, labeling and, according to his paperwork, shipping to a chain of gift shops out west.

He watched the forklift driver take it away, then dropped an empty pallet in its place. When he turned to retrieve the paperwork to ready the next shipment, the warehouse manager was walking toward him. Tom Voss was an older gentleman with a relaxed posture and easy smile. But that laid-back air was deceiving. He ran a tight ship and didn't put up with any slacking off.

Tom's ever-present smile widened. "How's it going?"

"Great. I've almost made it through my first day. I don't know if I've accomplished everything you wanted me to, but my body thinks so."

Tom laughed and slapped him roughly on the back. "No problem there. You're way ahead of where we expect someone to be on their first day. I'm impressed."

Shane raised his brows. The job wasn't exactly brain surgery. Anyone who could count and match item numbers and descriptions could do it. "Thanks for the compliment."

"It's well-deserved."

Tom had just started to walk away when Spike came through the swinging double doors twenty feet from where they stood. It was the first he had been around all day. He made a beeline for Tom, his gait that of someone with important business on his mind. He had almost reached his target when his gaze drifted past Tom. His eyes narrowed.

Yep, just what Shane expected. Spike had no knowledge of the hiring of Driggers' newest employee. And he obviously wasn't pleased. He fixed his dark eyes on Tom and nodded toward the other end of the warehouse. Well, not really nodded. More like an almost imperceptible tilt of his head. No one else would have noticed.

But Shane did. It was his job to pick up on the little nuances that others missed.

He slipped behind a group of pallets, some product that had arrived but not yet made it to the manufacturing end of the operation. Then he slunk along the wall, staying out of sight, except for brief periods when he had to sprint between pallets.

"Who hired him?" Spike's voice carried over the beeping of a forklift backing nearby, and Shane poked his head around the pallet. From his vantage point, both men stood in profile, facing one another.

"I did."

"Well, get rid of him." He issued the command in that authoritarian style that was popular in the fifties. Someone needed to tell him it didn't work so well in the twenty-first century.

"Why? He's doing a great job."

"I don't care what kind of job he's doing. I don't want him here."

"I don't have a reason to let him go." Tom dug in his heels with a stubbornness that seemed at odds with the easygoing manager who had made his regular rounds through the warehouse.

"You don't need a reason."

"What have you got against the guy?"

"Let's just say I don't like the way he looks. So get rid of him. If he's not gone by the end of the week, I'll take care of it myself, and you'll both be gone."

Tom stood in silence for several moments, fists

clenched. Then, without a word, he spun on his heel and started to stalk away.

Spike continued. "And Tom, one more thing."

Tom stopped walking but didn't turn around.

"From now on, all hiring decisions will go through me."

Now he did turn around. That warm, friendly air had disappeared. He was all tension, barely restrained temper. "Sonny, I've been doing all the hiring for Driggers Porcelain since you were in diapers. And I never had to clear a candidate with your father."

"Well, things have changed. You don't work for my father anymore." Spike turned and walked away, not giving Tom an opportunity to respond.

Shane returned to his area at a half jog. It wouldn't be good if he got caught eavesdropping. But either way, his time was short. He had four days at the most. Maybe as little as one.

When the bell rang at four, the other workers scrambled to put away assigned tools and gather keys and lunchboxes, but Shane hung back. There was only one reason Spike wanted him gone. There was something at Driggers Porcelain that he didn't want him to see.

He had already gotten well-acquainted with the shipping and receiving areas. During his morning and afternoon breaks, while several of his co-workers slipped outside to smoke, he had wandered around the warehouse familiarizing himself with the layout, listening to conversations and taking in what he could.

According to one of his coworkers, Driggers also ran a night shift. Those employees reported to work at five in the afternoon, just a skeleton crew. They handled special projects. When Shane pressed, the guy couldn't tell him what qualified as a special project.

Another interesting tidbit he had learned was that the factory had its own airstrip. Evidently Carlton Driggers had been a hobby pilot and had the strip installed years ago. If the Driggers brothers were involved in drug running, they had the ideal way to get their shipments in and out.

Shane pushed open one of three sets of metal doors leading out of the warehouse. According to what he had been told, down that wide, short hall was the heart of the operation, where the porcelain was manufactured. Each side wall was broken by a single closed door. Closets, maybe? They weren't offices. The doors weren't labeled. As far as he knew, all the offices were in the front, lining both sides of a long hall off the lobby.

He tried the first door. It was locked. He moved farther down the hall, toward the door on the opposite wall. As he started to reach for the knob, a muffled male voice penetrated the metal door. He flattened himself against the wall.

"Be careful with the boxes this time." The voice belonged to Spike. And it wasn't an instructional tone. More like scolding, implying a previous mistake.

"Sure, boss. But that last one wasn't all my fault. It got separated from the others and left behind. Then someone else picked it up."

"It was marked. You weren't paying attention to what you were doing."

"It's all right. We got everything put back where it should've been before it was all over."

Shane tried to place the voice, but it didn't belong to any of the employees he had met. It was raspy, with a hint of a New England accent, noticeable in the way he dropped the ending *r*.

"Yeah, but it could have turned out much worse. Just remember, I'm not going to tolerate any more mistakes from you."

"What, are you going to do me like we did the girl?" The laugh he emitted was more sarcasm than humor. "That'll never happen. You need me to do your dirty work."

"No one is indispensable. And don't you forget it."

The metallic scrape of the knob turning spurred Shane to action. He shot the final eight feet down the hall and disappeared through the double doors at its end.

Two men looked back at him, brows raised. They stood at a huge kiln. Judging from the rows of vases on the long table next to them, they had just finished firing some product.

Shane's gaze circled the room. "I'm looking for Tom. I guess he didn't come this way after all."

"No, we haven't seen him."

"This is pretty fascinating." He nodded toward all the equipment, most of which he didn't recognize. The kilns were obvious. So were the crushers and mills. The other pieces he could only make a wild guess as to their use. He should probably read up on the porcelain-making process.

But right now, he had time to kill. If Spike was still in that hall when he stepped out, he would be gone long before the end of the week.

"I work in shipping, but I'd love to see all this in action someday."

One of the men turned to face him fully. Donald, according to the embroidered patch over his right shirt pocket. "They do tours. I see them come around every so often, bringing people through and explaining the process step by step."

Shane nodded. "I'll have to watch for that."

Now finished, both men took jackets from hooks on the wall and made their way to the door. Shane fell in beside them, hoping the occupants of the room down the hall were gone. When they passed the first door, he breathed a sigh of relief. The room was quiet. Spike and his reprimanded employee— or whatever he was—had left.

What kind of mistake had the man with the raspy

voice made? And what kind of dirty work did he do? Was it related to the porcelain business, or something more diabolical? Was Spike's parting comment a threat to end the guy's employment, or his life?

And who was the girl the other man referred to, an employee?

Or his brother's nosy girlfriend?

EIGHT

Suds crept up the stainless steel sides of the sink as it filled, and Jessica added a plate and glass to the pot already there. Her latest book sat on the table, waiting for her to finish the dishes. It was light-hearted and fun, with a fast-moving, albeit shallow plot. Not her usual choice of reading material. But thrillers and murder mysteries didn't hold the appeal they used to. Living it took the fun out of reading about it.

She had just started washing when her KP duties were halted by an annoyingly familiar tune. It was that factory ringtone that, when it went off at the store, sent a half dozen people scrambling for their phones. She would change it eventually. She just hadn't gotten around to it.

She pulled the phone from her purse and glanced at the screen before pressing it to her ear. She didn't recognize the number. But she would never forget the Harmony Grove exchange.

"It's Lexi." The voice that came through the

phone was taut, with a heavy undercurrent of fear. "I think someone's watching me."

Jessica tensed. In light of everything she was learning about Priscilla, that couldn't be good. "What do you mean?"

"At first I thought it was my imagination. I mean, having the house broken into kind of set us all on edge."

"You were robbed?" She hadn't said anything about that.

"Not really robbed." She drew in a jagged breath. "It was the day after we found out about Priscilla. I finished class and made it home before Mom and Dad did. When I walked in, everything was a mess."

Uneasiness sifted over her, and even though she knew the answer, she had to ask. "A mess as in vandalized, or a mess as in ransacked?"

"Ransacked. They turned almost the whole place upside down. But they left my parents' room alone. So I think it was aimed at me."

"Was anything missing?"

"Not that I could tell." She sucked in another breath, then continued, her voice low. "I heard the same thing happened at Prissy's place. Do you think it's connected?"

"I don't know." It was too coincidental not to be. What did Lexi have to do with the whole ugly mess? Maybe nothing. But did Prissy's killer know that?

"You started to tell me you think you're being watched."

"Yeah. I keep seeing this same car. Yesterday it followed me all the way to school. Stayed a few car lengths behind me right up until I turned into the parking lot of Polk State."

"What kind of car?" Jess glanced at the window over the sink, suddenly feeling vulnerable. The other blinds in the house were closed, even the ones over the sliding glass doors. But she had opened the kitchen window blinds to let in some natural light while she cooked dinner.

"It's a dark gray four-door, not new but not really old, either." She gave a nervous laugh. "I guess I don't make a very good eyewitness."

"I take it the car isn't familiar." She reached for the wand to close the blinds. It was totally dark outside, the moon and stars obscured by the heavy layer of clouds that had begun to roll in at dusk.

"Not at all. It never gets close enough for me to see a hood emblem or anything."

Jessica pursed her lips. Why would someone follow Lexi? Were they afraid she knew too much? If so, she wouldn't be much safer than Priscilla was. Jessica dropped the wand and switched the phone to her other ear. But before she could move away, the phone slipped from her hand and landed in the sink with a spray of water and suds. She gasped in horror but didn't hesitate. In one fluid motion, she snatched the phone from its sudsy bath, snapped the battery from the back and grabbed a dry towel. If it didn't short out, maybe by tomorrow afternoon it would be thoroughly dry and operational.

But that didn't help her tonight. She needed to reach Lexi. Between the startled gasp and the dead phone, Lexi was probably half-crazy, thinking the worst.

Prissy's phone. It was still on the nightstand where she had dropped it after looking at the pictures on Shane's computer. She ran to the bedroom, powered it up and scrolled to Lexi Home. Halfway through the first ring, Lexi grabbed it. Jessica hurried to explain.

"So anyway, I'm hoping I haven't killed it. Meanwhile, I'm hanging on to Prissy's phone for another day or two." She strolled down the hall and plopped onto the living room couch. "You were talking about being followed."

"Yeah. Today I stopped to talk to Alan, and when I was walking back to my car, I saw that gray sedan parked about a block away. It looked as if there was just one person in it, the driver, but with the distance and the tinted windows, I have no idea who it was."

"Was that what you were talking to Alan about?"

"No, I haven't told Alan. Maybe I should. We've just chatted about personal stuff, you know."

Yeah, she did know. Lexi's whole tone changed when she talked about Alan. She sounded pretty enamored. She probably had plenty of company.

"You need to tell him. He can keep his eyes open, maybe figure out who this creep is and what he wants."

"I think I'll do that. I feel better already."

Jessica ended the call and returned to the dishes. But her thoughts didn't leave Lexi. What did they want with her? Lexi was a nice kid. Sweet, kind-hearted and a little naive.

And not at all equipped to deal with whatever mess Prissy had gotten her into.

Pounding drums and piercing guitars streamed into Jessica's room, jarring her from a sound sleep. Her eyes shot open and she lay frozen in the darkness. The radio was on. Someone was inside. Panic limped up her spine, and her heart pounded against her rib cage, sending the blood roaring through her ears.

Within moments, the music stopped, and a tension-filled silence permeated the house. Reason slowly filtered in as the grogginess of sleep dissipated. That was no radio. It was a cell phone. Prissy's phone. She thrust back the covers and jumped from the bed. If she decided to keep the phone, that would be an immediate change—no obnoxious ringtones.

She sprinted to the living room, picked up the phone from the end table and squinted at the display. Lexi Cell. She better have a really good reason for a 1:00 a.m. call.

She pressed the screen to redial.

"Jessica?"

It was Lexi. But her tone was several pitches higher than normal and laced with hysteria. Jessica gripped the phone more tightly, the last traces of sleep fleeing her brain.

"Lexi, what's wrong?"

"Oh, Jessie, I'm so scar—"

Her panicked words were cut off by rustling, as if she was moving around with the phone.

Or someone was taking it from her.

"Lexi, what's going on?"

"Listen carefully." The raspy male voice wasn't familiar, but the slight accent was. She knew someone with that same accent. A woman. Rhode Island. That was it. For a short time, Jessica worked with a girl who had recently moved from Rhode Island. She spoke the same way, ignored the ending *r's* in her words.

"I'm listening."

"Come to the park, and bring your sister's phone. Leave it on the bench at the east end of the lake. Then walk back to your car. If you're getting any ideas about trying to be a hero, get rid of them.

Come alone. Don't call the police. And don't try anything. Or sweet little Lexi here will meet a not-very-pleasant end." The line clicked dead.

Jessica flew into action, her mind ticking through her options. If she could bring down the caller, maybe she could get some answers. But she probably couldn't do it alone, especially if he was armed. She could call Shane, or even Alan or Tommy. But the caller had warned her. Bad things would happen to Lexi if he found out. No, that wasn't a chance she was willing to take.

She threw a light jacket over her PJs and hurried to her car, thankful that C.J. had finished the brakes. When she reached the park and stepped into the night air, a shiver passed through her. It wasn't cold. The temperature was that same sixties low that had given Florida its paradise reputation. But there was something disconcerting about strolling through a deserted park in the dead of night. Swings swayed in a barely there breeze, and the street lamps scattered throughout the park struggled to hold back the heavy darkness.

She moved toward the lake, scanning her surroundings for any sign of movement. The whole thing could be a trap, the order to bring the phone nothing but a ploy to get her alone. But it was a chance she would have to take. She wasn't going to put Lexi's life at risk for her own safety.

She approached the bench, every muscle coiled,

ready to spring. As instructed, she had come alone. But she wouldn't go down without a fight.

As she laid the phone on the varnished wooden slats, she kept her head up, her eyes peeled and her mind alert. He was there. She couldn't see or hear him, but he was watching. She could feel it.

She straightened and backed away from the bench. He had instructed her to walk back to her car. But where was Lexi? Would he let her go once he had the phone?

No, she couldn't leave. Not until she knew Lexi was safe.

"I've left you the phone." Her voice pierced the silence of the park, filled with a confidence she didn't feel. "I've done what you asked. So let Lexi go."

There was no response. Maybe she needed to give him more space. She backed away, putting a good thirty yards between herself and the bench where the phone still sat untouched.

A figure stepped out clumsily from behind one of the huge oaks and limped toward the bench. As it moved from the shadows into the soft glow of the street lamp, she knew. That wasn't a single figure. It was two people, the taller one shielding himself with the body of the smaller one.

And that smaller figure was Lexi. Dim yellow light washed over her, casting her long blond hair and pale skin in a soft glow. Her eyes weren't visible. But Jessica didn't need to see them to know they were wide and filled with fear.

The larger figure reached for the phone, but instead of releasing Lexi, began to drag her back the way they had come.

A seed of panic sprouted in Jessica's chest. She hadn't thought far enough ahead to come up with a plan if her caller didn't keep his side of the bargain.

"Let her go." The command rang out strong and sharp. She had followed his instructions explicitly. Well, all except returning to her car. But he had what he wanted. And she wasn't going to let him drag Lexi away.

"Let her go," she commanded again, with even more force. But she didn't wait for him to respond. She shot toward them at a full run.

The next moment, he thrust Lexi to the ground and disappeared into the shadows.

Jessica ran the final yards and dropped to her knees. "Are you all right?"

Lexi didn't answer, just dissolved into sobs and raised trembling hands to her face.

"It's okay. You're safe now." She gave her an awkward pat on the arm. She should be doing more to offer comfort. But she wasn't good at this kind of thing. What she really wanted to do was pump Lexi full of questions. How did her kidnapper know Jessica had Priscilla's phone? How did he know to go to Lexi in the first place?

"Come on," she coaxed, reining in her curiosity. "Take my hand, and I'll help you to my car."

Lexi complied, and by the time they reached the

Bug, she had stopped crying. She slid into the passenger's seat and drew in a shaky breath. "He had a knife. He said he was going to slice my throat open if I didn't cooperate." A shudder shook her shoulders, and she tipped her head back and closed her eyes.

A pang of tenderness wound its way through Jessica's heart. It would be a long time before Lexi would recover from the trauma of this night. "Do you know who he was?"

She shook her head. "He was wearing one of those knit ski masks. He broke into the house and clamped his hand over my mouth so I wouldn't wake up Mom and Dad. Then he dragged me outside and stuffed me into the trunk."

"What was he driving?"

"My dad's car. I guess he took the keys from the hook near the door. He wanted to know who called using Prissy's phone."

With a flash of clarity, all the pieces fell into place. When they ransacked Prissy's and Lexi's houses, they were looking for the phone. But it was in Lexi's car. Someone was watching Prissy's account, and the call to Lexi gave them just the break they needed.

Jessica cranked the car and looked over at Lexi. "We've got to report this to the police."

Lexi nodded.

If Branch investigated, he would probably ignore it, or at the least, minimize its importance. But she wasn't going to let it go. First thing in the morning, she would tell Shane. Because there was something significant on that phone, something someone wanted to keep a secret.

Enough to kill for.

Shane closed his Bible and rose from the table to place his cereal bowl and spoon in the sink. The dishes could wait until tonight. He still had his lunch to pack.

He turned toward the fridge as his cell phone rang. It was either Ross or Jess. No one except Jess called him in Harmony Grove. And other than his mom's weekly calls, hearing from someone back home was like one of those rare cosmic events. Of course, that was his fault. When he left home two and a half years ago, his friends tried to keep up the contact. He accepted their calls, just didn't initiate any of his own. Their calls got further apart and eventually stopped altogether. They probably got tired of one-sided relationships.

He pulled the phone from the pouch on his side and glanced at the screen before pressing it to his ear. "Hi, Jess, how are you?"

"A little tired, after my unexpected trip to the park in the middle of the night."

He froze midway to the fridge. "Why were you at the park in the middle of the night?"

"Someone wanted Prissy's phone. Badly enough to kidnap Lexi and hold her for ransom."

A giant fist clamped down on his stomach, twisting it painfully sideways. "You should have called me."

"I couldn't. The caller said to come alone. I wasn't about to risk getting Lexi killed."

"Instead you risked getting *yourself* killed." She probably didn't appreciate the scolding. But he couldn't help it. The thought of her being lured alone to a dark and deserted park just about made him crazy. "What if it had been a trap?"

"I thought of that. Still, I didn't have much choice. But it all worked out okay. I'm back home safe and sound."

Yes, she was all right. He breathed a silent prayer of thanks, refusing to think about all that could have happened. An unexpected longing filled him, a sudden driving need to see her, to touch her and hold her and make sure she was unharmed. He tamped it down and gave himself a silent scolding. Somehow when Jess was involved, professional objectivity took a hike.

He propped the phone against his ear with his shoulder and bent to rummage through the fridge, emerging with a loaf of bread, mayonnaise, some lunch meat and cheese. "Look, if anything like this happens again, call me. I'm trained. I know how to trail someone without being noticed." And what to do if things went horribly wrong.

She didn't make any promises. He didn't expect her to. If Jess was anything, she was honest. If the situation arose again, her choice would be the same. She would never put her own safety above someone else's.

"Just be careful, please."

"I will." She drew in a deep breath. "There was something important on that phone, and my gut tells me it's that photo we looked at on your computer, the one with Hammy and Spike and the mystery guy. You didn't happen to save it, did you?" Cautious optimism filled her tone.

He slathered some mayonnaise on two slices of bread. "Actually, I did."

"We need to find out who that third guy is."

"I've already got someone working on it."

"Good. My guess is since he was with Hammy and Spike when Prissy took the picture, he'll show up sooner or later, possibly at the factory."

"I'll keep my eyes open. But I don't know how long I'll be there. Spike wasn't pleased when he saw his newest employee."

"Uh-oh. Do you think he might get rid of you? Lay you off, I mean?"

He laughed. "Glad you clarified that. Yeah, I'm afraid my days are numbered. I overheard him tell the warehouse manager to make sure I'm gone by the end of the week."

"Oh, no, that was our in."

The disappointment in her voice tugged at his heart, and determination surged through him. Getting booted from Driggers would be a setback. But he wasn't giving up until both cases were solved. After all, it was his job. But it was more than that. For Jess, finding her sister's killer meant everything. And he was determined to make it happen for her, whatever it took.

As much as he tried to deny it, he was falling for her. She was tough, but beneath that tough facade was an underlying tenderness. It showed in her gentle touch when she wiped the blood from his face the night they met, in the way she cared for Buttons when the last thing she wanted was a dog, even in her determination to bring Priscilla's killer to justice. Life hadn't been kind to her, but she had somehow managed to bloom in spite of it.

"We'll find this guy, Jess. Whoever did this to your sister, he's not going to get away with it." He dropped the finished sandwich into a zippered plastic bag and washed an apple. "You didn't happen to see the guy at the park last night, did you?"

"No, I didn't get close enough. But Lexi said he was wearing a ski mask."

His grip on the phone tightened, and he stalked into the living room. He couldn't get the image out of his mind, Jessica alone and unprotected while a dangerous masked man waited in the shadows.

"Did you report all this to the police?"

"Oh, yeah. Not that it did any good, because I got Branch again. It's as if he knows when something has gone down and makes sure he's the one who takes the call. He always swaggers in with that touch of annoyance, as if we're bothering him with trivialities when he's got so much more important stuff to do. This time I told him if it's too much trouble for him to do a thorough investigation, I'll talk to Tommy or Alan."

Shane grimaced. Branch wouldn't take kindly to threats. Even if he did deserve them.

"Well," she said, "I better let you go so you're not late for work. I'd hate to give Spike a reason to fire you."

"I'm sure it wouldn't take much." He retrieved his keys from the coffee table and dropped them into his pocket. "How about coming over tonight for pizza and a movie. Something lighthearted and fun."

Several seconds passed while she considered his offer. "All right. I could use lighthearted and fun."

"Good. I'll meet you at BethAnn's at six."

"Shane?"

"Yeah?"

"Thanks."

"For what?"

"Everything. It's nice to have a friend, someone who doesn't judge me based on who I used to be."

"Same here."

"I *can't* judge you. I don't *know* who you used to be."

"I mean it's nice to have a friend."

"Yeah."

Disbelief laced her tone. She was right. It was

a pretty one-sided friendship. He knew all about her—her dysfunctional family, her troubled childhood, even her failed business. And what did she know about him? That he was an FBI agent, moved around a lot and was sort of writing a book. Nothing about his personal life or his past.

But why reopen old wounds? Why set his mind down that forbidden path and invite yet another nightmare? It would accomplish nothing. Because eventually, he would wrap up this case and move on to the next.

That was just the way it had to be.

No matter how solidly she was winding her way into his heart.

NINE

Jessica locked the door to BethAnn's and climbed into the front passenger seat of Shane's Denali.

"Mmm, smells yummy." She drew in a deep breath, savoring the enticing aroma.

Shane flashed her an apologetic smile and pulled away from the curb. "What you're smelling is bread-sticks and sauce. I arrived to pick up the pizza, and they had lost the order. They're a little swamped, but they promised to have it ready in forty minutes. Meanwhile, we can start the movie while we munch on breadsticks."

Rhythmic thumping from the backseat drew her attention, and she turned to see Buttons quivering with excitement, tail beating the seat with every wag.

"Well, come here, sweetie." She patted the seat beside her and looked over at Shane, brows raised.

He smiled back at her. "I've already taken him out and fed him. So he can just chill and watch the movie with us."

"Are you sure the Harrisons will be okay with that? Maybe they don't allow pets."

"They don't. But I got special permission for tonight."

Warmth spread through her chest. Shane had thought of everything. Why did he have to be so perfect?

She cleared her throat and forced a nonchalant tone. "How did work go today? Are you still gainfully employed?"

"*I* am. Tom Voss isn't."

"Tom got fired?"

"I don't know if Spike fired him or he walked out. Based on what I overheard yesterday, Spike's strong-arm tactics didn't go over well. I wouldn't be surprised if Tom told him what he could do with the job." He pulled into the parking lot of Yesteryear Antiques and smiled over at her. "With Tom gone, I'll probably be next, but look at the bright side. I'll be free to walk you to work in the mornings again."

"You know, it's probably not necessary. I feel pretty safe in broad daylight."

He flashed her a teasing smile. "Getting tired of me?"

Tired of him? She would never get tired of walking next to him hand in hand, or his arm draped across her shoulders. Yeah, it was just for show. He had made that clear. But that didn't stop her from enjoying it.

She climbed from the seat and, after looping the

end of the leash over her hand, put Buttons on the ground and made her way around the front of the vehicle. "I just don't want you to feel obligated, like you have to protect me. If there's something else you need to do, go ahead. I do pretty well taking care of myself."

"I don't doubt that for a second. But humor me. Us guys, we *like* to be protectors. It's the way God wired us. You know, the whole knight in shining armor thing."

No, she *didn't* know. "I thought 'knight in shining armor' was a Hollywood concept. I can't say that I've ever seen it in real life." Most of the guys she had known were more interested in using her than protecting her.

She moved past him, but Shane snagged her hand, pulling her to a stop.

"Then you've been associating with the wrong kind of men."

When she turned to face him, his expression was serious, his gaze filled with meaning. In the fading afternoon light, his eyes had darkened to a deep hazel, the gold flecks no longer distinguishable. The warmth there touched something deep inside her, and an unexpected sense of longing gripped her heart.

She pulled her hand free and headed toward the stairs leading to his apartment. He was probably right. She probably *had* been associating with the wrong kind of men. But she didn't know there was more than one type. Until Shane. He had done so much for her but expected nothing in return. With her past as a backdrop, he seemed too good to be true.

Actually, he was. Because whatever secrets he was keeping, whatever he was running from, he would never be hers.

She shrugged off the thought. Feeling sorry for herself was a pointless waste of time. There were a whole lot more productive ways to expend her energy. Like trying to find her sister's killer.

She cast a glance back at Shane coming up the stairs behind her. "Did you get a chance to do any snooping today?"

"I did yesterday."

"Learn anything interesting?"

"Not yet. At least nothing that I can definitely connect to your sister." He shoved the key into the lock and turned. "I overheard Spike chewing out someone for some kind of mistake. The guy had a New England accent."

Her heart rate kicked up several notches. "So did the guy who called me last night."

"It's probably the same guy. There aren't too many New Englanders wandering around Harmony Grove." He swung open the door and motioned her inside.

Buttons bounded in first, and she followed. Shane's living area looked like it had the other time she was there. He was at least consistent. Not super neat, but definitely not a slob. A used mug sat on the end table, and a throw pillow had become wedged between the couch cushion and the edge of the couch, probably when Shane had sat there earlier. The Bible still lay on the coffee table, but this time it was open.

"Have a seat, and I'll get us some drinks." He set the box of breadsticks on the end table and headed toward the kitchen.

She moved around the front of the couch, curious about what he was reading. It was open to the book of Romans. Several lines had been shaded with a yellow highlighter, and tiny notes were scrawled in the margins. Shane took his religion seriously. He didn't just read the Bible. He studied it. Was his faith what made him different from the other men she had known?

The clink of ice against glass sounded in the kitchen, followed by the pop and hiss of two sodas being opened. She settled onto the couch, and Buttons snuggled in next to her, right at home. The apartment was cozy, the furnishings simple. Two end tables flanked the couch, and a matching love seat sat adjacent to it.

Shane returned with a glass of soda in each hand and a roll of paper towels stuffed under one arm. After popping the movie into the DVD player, he picked up the remote and sat next to her.

"I don't know if it's worth starting the movie, but I suppose we'll at least get through the credits."

They *did* get through the credits, along with the half dozen complimentary breadsticks Pappy's had offered as consolation for what would have been a wasted trip. Shane stood and pulled his keys from his pocket. "I'll be back in a flash. You and Buttons can just hang out if you'd like."

As soon as Shane left, Jessica took the opportunity to lay her head back and rest. Now that she had sat still for some time, last night's lack of sleep was starting to catch up with her. A ten-minute power nap would go a long way toward keeping her awake through the rest of the movie.

The nap was not to be. She had no sooner closed her eyes when music cut through the silence of the apartment, that same factory ringtone. When her phone was still dead at lunchtime, she had let Beth-Ann man the store while she ran out to pick up the cheapest replacement she could find. No way was she going to sleep alone in the house, cut off from the outside world.

She put the phone to her ear. It was BethAnn. In labor.

"We're headed to the hospital. I'm a little concerned, because it's about three weeks early."

"Don't worry about anything at the store. I'll hold down the fort."

"I need you to place an order for me. I was going to do it today but ran out of time."

She rose from the couch and headed toward Shane's desk. BethAnn was in labor and on her way to the hospital, and she was worrying about stock. Jessica smiled. As a former business owner herself, she could relate.

She pulled a sheet of clean paper from the printer and opened the top desk drawer in search of a pen. Two lay next to some file folders. "Okay. Shoot."

After completing the eight-item list, she dropped the pen back into the drawer and wished BethAnn luck. She had slid the drawer halfway closed when her eyes fell on the file folder tab. Parker. The reports on Prissy's case. Shane had already told her what was in them. He had even offered to make her copies of the police and autopsy reports. He just hadn't gotten around to it yet.

She picked up the folder and held it for several moments before opening it. Shane would have a problem with her seeing what was inside only if he was keeping something from her. If he *was* keeping something from her, she had a right to know what.

She laid the folder on the desk and flipped it open. The first three pages contained information on the purchase of the Lotus, followed by a banking transaction list. Prissy's checking account. Shane had told her about the suspicious deposits. Seeing them for herself made it all the more real. Those kinds of deposits didn't come from waiting tables. Was Prissy blackmailing someone? Hammy? Spike?

The last items were the autopsy report and the police report, the same ones Alan had shown her. She closed the folder, relief coursing through her.

Shane had been totally honest. Trust for her didn't come easily. But she had found herself wanting to trust him almost from the start. For once it wasn't misplaced.

She started to put the file back into the drawer. Another file lay there, this one labeled Background Checks. Shane didn't mention those. He probably had checks run on Hammy and Spike. She removed and opened the file. On top was a criminal history for Wilford Driggers. Spike. She knew because of the picture. Evidently his real name was a well-kept secret. She scanned the pages, three in all. He had been arrested for possession and a couple of burglaries. His report was surprisingly short.

The next one wasn't. It was a minibook and belonged to Thaddeus Driggers. Hammy. She smiled wryly. Wilford and Thaddeus. They sounded like a couple of accountants.

She picked up the thick stack of pages. Skimming Hammy's criminal history was out of the question. Shane would be back long before she finished. Hammy hadn't just followed in his big brother's footsteps; he approached getting in trouble as if it was a contest and he was going for the gold.

She slid the stack of pages aside, and her jaw went slack. The face that stared back at her was her own. Shane had ordered a criminal history on her. While he pretended to be her friend, he was having her investigated. While he talked about working as a team, he viewed her as little more than another possible suspect.

A sudden coldness filled her core and spread outward to her limbs. She was right. Shane *was* too good to be true. His words of trust were nothing but a lie. She had been snookered again.

With Daryl, she had blindly swallowed his sweet words while he cleaned out her bank account and ran her business into the ground. Unfortunately, she didn't learn her lesson. Because here it was, nine months later, and she had bought a ticket on that same train. She had dropped her guard and let Shane touch her heart, believing he cared for her, when all she was to him was a source of information.

What was wrong with her? Did she crave companionship so badly that she made an easy target for the con men of the world? Was she really that pathetic?

She slapped the folder closed and rose from the chair. Fine. He could go ahead with his investigation. He would even have her cooperation, because she would do anything to find Prissy's killer.

He didn't have to lie.

Or pretend something he didn't feel.

"Pizza delivery."

Shane pushed the door shut with his shoulder and looked around the room. "Jess?"

Dread trickled over him, and a cold knot of fear

formed in his stomach. Where was she? Maybe she went to the bathroom. The door was closed. Of course, it was closed when he left, too. He moved farther into the room and set the box of pizza on the coffee table. If she went to the bathroom, Buttons went with her.

He sat down on the couch and waited, but everything was quiet. Too quiet. After another minute, he crossed the room and rapped lightly on the closed door. "Jess?"

Nothing. The dread intensified, gradually turning to panic. What happened to her? It was as if she had disappeared into thin air, Buttons with her. He was only gone ten minutes, fifteen tops. And he had locked the door on his way out. Did someone come in during that brief period and take her away?

No, that was impossible. Tangling with Jess usually involved broken wood and shattered glass. But there wasn't a lamp, chair or couch cushion disturbed. His gaze circled the room until it came to rest on his desk. The top drawer was open a half inch. His confusion gave way to annoyance. Was she snooping through his things while he was gone? Did something tick her off enough that she left?

There was nothing in that drawer except some office supplies, a notepad and the two files on the Priscilla Parker case. He hadn't bothered to move the files, because there was nothing to hide. He had already told her everything he had learned. So what was her problem?

He flew down the stairs and charged across the street. Just as he thought. She was home. The living room shades were drawn, but slivers of light squeezed out around their perimeter. He knocked on the door and was mildly surprised when it opened right away. Jess stood with one fist pressed into the curve of her waist, the other hand gripping the doorknob. Definitely a you've-ticked-me-off stance.

Noncombative would probably be the best way to start. He gave her a tentative smile. "There's a pizza and an unfinished movie waiting across the street."

"Let's just drop the pretense, okay?"

He raised his brows at the sarcasm in her tone. Maybe he was a little thickheaded, but she was going to have to spell it out. "What are you talking about?"

"Look, I'm going to work with you on the case. I'm willing to talk to everyone I possibly can and share everything I learn with you, simply because I want my sister's killer caught as badly as you do. I'm giving you what you want. So don't pretend that we have any kind of friendship going on."

Her explanation left him more confused than ever. "I'm not pretending anything. We *do* have a friendship, at least on my end."

"Oh, please." Her tone was thick with sarcasm.

"Can I come in?" If they were going to have an argument, he preferred for it to happen inside the house, away from any curious ears.

She backed away, and once inside, he closed the door behind him.

"You're going to have to explain to me what has set you off, because frankly, I don't have a clue."

"I looked at the stuff you have on my sister."

"I know. I could tell you got into my desk."

She raised her chin. "I had to borrow a pen."

"And that entailed going through my files?" He tried to temper the annoyance still churning in his chest. He had taken her into his confidence. And she betrayed that trust by snooping through his apartment as soon as he walked out the door.

"I didn't think it would be a problem, because you supposedly told me everything."

"I *did* tell you everything."

"Background checks?"

"We always check out possible suspects." As soon as the words were out of his mouth, he wished he could draw them back. It wasn't Hammy and Spike's background checks she was upset about. It was her own. He should have destroyed that report as soon as he read it, or better yet, not even printed it.

"Exactly what I thought. Suspects."

"I didn't mean you." He stepped forward to put a hand on her arm, but she shook off his touch.

"Do you really expect me to believe that?"

"Okay. At first I didn't know what to think. I watched you break into the house with a screwdriver. I had no idea whether you had any involvement in this mess or not."

She turned and started to pace. "I don't have a problem with that. What I have a problem with is being used—your talking about trust when there isn't any, and pretending friendship when I'm nothing more than another suspect, or a good source of information." She spun to face him, arms crossed in front of her. "Lying is what I have a problem with. I may not be perfect, but at least I'm honest. You know exactly where you stand with me. That's more than I can say for you. And any other man I've met." She heaved a sigh. "I thought you were different."

The disappointment in her tone shot straight to his heart. She had suffered a lot at the hands of men. Three "fathers" who made a mockery of the word. The creep that used her to help him commit his crimes. The lowlife that wove his way into her heart then milked her business dry. And probably some others in between that she hadn't mentioned.

He stepped closer and rested a hand on her shoulder. He *wasn't* like the other men she had known. Somehow he had to make her see that. "When I said I trusted you, I meant it. I had your background check run after knowing you for just two days. Since then I've not only come to trust you, I've come to consider you a good friend."

Her eyes raked over him. "I don't believe you."

He put both hands on her shoulders. This time she didn't pull away.

"I know you've had more than your fair share of men who did nothing more than use you. I'm not like that. I believe in treating women with respect, protecting and cherishing them. Right from the start, I've admired your resilience and honesty and strength. I care about you, Jess."

She pushed him back against the wall and gently held him there, her gaze earnest. "If you care about me, then prove it."

His eyes dipped to her mouth. She was inches away. Close enough to kiss. He silently chided himself for the direction his thoughts had gone. As badly as he wanted to kiss her, that probably wasn't what she meant.

"Open up to me."

His eyes snapped back up to meet hers. "What do you mean?"

"Tell me what you're running from."

He lowered his gaze. "I'm not running from anything. I don't form emotional attachments because I move around too much. It's all part of the job. And it suits me fine." No, that wasn't even true. Because no matter how many years he ran from the memories, he would always long for the warmth and stability of home.

"I don't believe you."

He avoided her eyes, but couldn't ignore her scent, clean and fresh, slightly floral and totally feminine. It scattered his thoughts, sending them spiraling off in a thousand different directions.

She leaned even closer, shattering what little concentration he had left. "Tell me the truth. What are you running from?" Her voice was smooth and low, and it flowed over him like sweet, scented oil, soothing the raw places in his heart.

He shook his head. To talk about it was to relive it. And he did enough of that in his dreams.

But then he met her gaze, filled with understanding, not of his circumstances, but his pain. And the words he had refused to form tumbled out anyway.

"I lost someone close to me. She was murdered."

"I'm so sorry. How long ago?"

"Three years." For six months, he stayed and walked around in a grief-induced fog. Then he joined the Bureau and took off. And at times, he still moved about in a grief-induced fog.

She reached up to cup his face with both hands. "You can't go through the rest of your life afraid to love again. Maybe it's time to stop running."

She dropped her hands and stepped away, and he gave her a small nod.

But it was more complicated than that. It wasn't just the loss. It was the guilt, knowing that the only reason he was still alive was because she was dead. And the determination that, no matter what, it would never happen again.

He could quit the FBI, leave police work altogether. But it was his calling. It was what he did. And maybe, because of his efforts, a teenager was preparing to walk at his high school graduation, a young woman was able to face life without looking over her shoulder and a husband was around to love his wife another day.

He couldn't undo his own past. But he could change the future for others.

TEN

Jessica pushed herself away from the table. Three candles burned in the center, surrounded by empty dishes that, an hour ago, had held meatloaf, mashed potatoes and green beans. Her cooking wasn't fancy, but it was substantial.

Shane had walked her home, and though their conversation had remained lighthearted, something had changed, at least for her. The carefree roamer had a tragic past. For some reason, that made him all the more attractive. The next thing she knew, she was inviting him to dinner.

Shane rose and gathered their dishes. "Let me help you clean up the mess. Then I'll leave so you can get some sleep, since we both have to get up and go to work tomorrow."

She added two squirts of dish soap to the sink. "I'm surprised you're still employed."

"Me, too. I'm just not getting much investigating done. I keep bumping into Hammy."

"Well, I've been doing some calling around, trying to find the man with the New England accent, but I'm not having much luck. Seems no one's heard of him."

Frowning, he rinsed the pan she had washed and placed it in the drainer with the dripping plates already there. "Be careful who you ask. You don't want it to get back to the wrong people."

"Don't worry, I'm being stealthy. I've just asked a few people who came into the store, and yesterday afternoon I called Driggers."

He raised his brows. "That's your definition of stealth?"

"Not Hammy and Spike. The factory. BethAnn told me that Sandy Cutchins works in HR at Driggers. She was a couple years behind me in school, but I knew she'd remember me. Anyhow, I figured if he's an employee, she'd know."

"And did she?"

"No. But she was going to ask around the factory." She dried her hands and bent to pick up Buttons while Shane put away the last of the dishes.

"It looks as if he's growing on you."

Jessica smiled. Large brown eyes gazed back at her, filled with adoration. "Yeah, he is. I'm actually thinking of keeping him."

She must have lost her mind. As unsettled as her life was, the last thing she needed was a dog. But she couldn't bring herself to take him to the shelter. He had been through enough in his short life. Besides, it was the last thing she could do for Prissy.

She set him on the couch and walked with Shane to the door. The warmth in his smile was reflected in his eyes.

"Thanks for dinner. I enjoyed it."

"Me, too. I still owe you two meals. If you remember, you've taken me to Pappy's twice. Plus, there was last night's dinner and movie." She did end up going back to Shane's to finish both.

"You don't owe me, but I certainly won't turn you down."

He stepped onto the porch and turned to face her. "Thanks again. I'm looking forward to next time. And when it's my turn, we'll scope out the restaurants. I won't be inviting you to my place for a home-cooked meal unless you're fond of frozen dinners."

"Dinner out sounds wonderful." So did frozen dinners. Peanut butter and jelly had appeal if Shane was nearby. Especially when he was looking at her the way he was now. His smile had faded and he had leaned in, eyes soft with emotion, lips parted. As if he wanted to kiss her.

Instead, he swallowed hard, squeezed her shoulder and turned to walk down the driveway. As she watched his masculine form disappear into the darkness, disappointment settled in her chest. She hadn't imagined it. He had wanted to kiss her. Her track record for choosing good men was terrible, but she knew when a man was attracted to her. And Shane was.

But he was also someone who would never commit. He was honorable. He wouldn't play with her heart. But if he had wanted a good-night kiss, she wouldn't have minded. Not at all.

She closed the door with a sigh and turned off the living room lights. It was too early to go to sleep. Instead, she would pick up the lighthearted read she had started a few days ago.

She had just settled into bed, Buttons snuggled up next to her, when her phone rang. She stretched across the nightstand to pull it from her purse. The number displayed on the screen was unfamiliar, and a shiver of uneasiness passed through her. She breathed a tentative "Hello."

"Jess, it's Sandy. I hope it's not too late to call. We had dinner out and just got home."

All the uneasiness was swept aside by a wave of anticipation. "No, not at all. Any luck identifying the mystery man?"

"Maybe. No one seemed to know anything. Then I talked to Denise, Spike's secretary. She's taken several calls from a Nick Lombardi, who she said talks like a New Yorker. She said a lot of times Spike puts people off, but never Nick. Nick's calls always go straight through."

She fished through her purse for a pen and paper and jotted down the name. "Did she have any idea what their relationship is?"

"She didn't know. She's never met him in person, and she's never handled any kind of paperwork. Whatever dealings they've had, Spike hasn't involved her."

"Interesting. Anything else?"

"No, except Spike walked in at the end of our conversation, and he didn't look too happy. Even though I was on my afternoon break, he said I needed to get back to work."

Great. Just what she *didn't* want to happen. And what Shane had warned her about. "Well, thanks for asking for me."

"No problem. I'm glad to help you out. I was hired by Carlton right out of high school, and my loyalties are to him. His sons give me the creeps."

"Yeah, me, too. If you find out anything else, let me know."

After disconnecting the call, she held the phone in her hand for several moments. Shane probably wasn't asleep yet. He had been gone for only thirty minutes.

Decision made, she touched the screen three times and put the phone to her ear. She had a name. Maybe Shane could fill in the rest of the blanks.

He answered on the second ring, and she relayed the details of the conversation. "So do you think you might be able to find out who he is?"

"Possibly. Although it would help if we had an approximate age. Do you know how many Nick Lombardis there are in the New England area?"

"Probably a lot. But at least it's somewhere to start."

"I'll get on it tomorrow."

As she disconnected the call, the crack of shattering glass pierced the still night, and her heart almost stopped. Panic ricocheted through her system, threatening to paralyze her. But whatever threat was invading her home, no way was she going to cower in bed and wait for it.

Buttons sailed to the floor in the midst of a barking frenzy, and Jessica flew to her feet. By the time her intruder climbed through the window, she would be ready to meet him…with Prissy's pistol. She snatched the gun from its hiding place at the bottom of her T-shirt drawer and slipped from the room, trying to remember everything she had ever heard about handling a gun. Hopefully just the sight would be enough to keep her intruder outside.

She stopped at the edge of the living room, her gaze falling on the front window. Four of the vertical blind slats had been yanked loose and lay on the floor. Jagged shards of glass jutted from the window frame, glistening in the moonlight. The porch light was out, the bulb probably removed by whoever broke the window. The rest of the glass littered the carpet, and a burlap sack lay in the middle of the room. A *moving* burlap sack.

She reached for the light switch, and crisp white light chased away the last of the shadows. Buttons stood beside her, barking for all he was worth, but unwilling to leave the safety of her side. She cocked the gun and waited. The top of the bag was open, whatever was inside making its way out. A head emerged, dry and scaly, with two beady black eyes. A forked tongue shot from the mouth, wiggling in a sinister little dance before disappearing back inside.

Cold terror washed over her. Not a snake. Anything but a snake.

She aimed, closed her eyes and squeezed the trigger. The resultant explosion and shattering glass wrenched a startled shriek from her throat. The bullet had ricocheted and taken out the TV. The snake was unharmed. It was almost out of the bag now. It slithered onto the living room carpet, exposing its brown diamond-shaped patterns inch by inch. Within moments, the telltale rattle confirmed her fears.

She had to kill it. And the gun wasn't a good option. Something with a long handle. She mentally ticked through the contents of the bedroom closets. Nothing but a set of crutches. She scooped up Buttons and bolted into the first bedroom. Seconds later, she stepped back into the hall, weapon in hand, and slammed the door. Buttons renewed his barking, voicing his objections at being closed up. But she had enough on her mind without worrying about Prissy's dog.

She gripped the bottom of the crutch with both hands, and the snake drew into a coil and raised its head. The warning hiss and rattle sent tendrils of fear crawling up her spine. She raised the crutch and, with a strangled scream, swung downward, fast and sharp. Again and again she swung, hysteria urging her on. Finally, a soothing male voice penetrated the fog.

"Jess, I think it's dead."

She stared in confusion at the broken window. Shane stood just outside.

"Come on, open the door. Let me in."

She still stood frozen, her brain unable to process his request. A quivery weakness settled in her knees and climbed upward, spreading all the way to her fingertips. Finally, she stumbled toward the front door, giving the snake wide berth, and threw the locks.

"What took you so long?" Her voice was several pitches higher than normal, and she fought back an irrational urge to grab and shake him.

"I heard a gunshot and ran right over." He stepped inside and pushed the door shut, his gaze flicking to the demolished TV. "Are you all right?"

"No, I'm not all right." Her tone was still tinged with hysteria. She *wasn't* all right, and wouldn't be for a long time.

"It's okay. You're safe now."

He continued in the same soothing tone, as if trying to calm a frightened child. It wasn't working.

"I don't think you need this anymore."

She followed his gaze to her left hand, which still maintained a death grip on the metal bottom of the crutch. He reached for the item, and she released it one finger at a time, unable to relinquish the makeshift weapon all at once. She hated snakes. It didn't matter what kind. Poisonous, harmless, large or small. The only good snake was a dead snake.

A shudder shook her shoulders, and he drew her into the circle of his arms. Barefoot, she didn't even reach his chin. But that was all right. His height was perfect. With his strong arms wrapped around her and her face pressed to that muscular chest, she felt sheltered and protected. It was a new experience, and she wanted to hang on to it forever.

All too soon, he pulled away. "Let me get rid of that so you don't have to look at it."

He opened the front door, then slid the crutch under the center of the snake. A minute later he was back. Hopefully he disposed of it in his own trash can.

He gave her shoulder a squeeze. "Are you going to be okay?"

She bobbed her head and swallowed hard. Because she suddenly felt as if she was going to cry. No way. She didn't cry when Buck beat her up. She didn't cry when Daryl cleaned her out. She didn't even cry when she found out Prissy was dead. She wasn't going to cry over a stupid snake.

"I'm fine." She forced the words through a constricted throat. "Just shaken up. I hate snakes."

"I can tell." A smile quivered at the corners of his mouth. "You killed the TV."

"I know." That really stank. It was a big-screen LED TV, something she'd never be able to replace. Maybe if she didn't eat for a year. "I'll bring out the one from the spare bedroom." It was much smaller, but it was better than nothing.

Shane shook his head, the repressed smile still there. "I can't believe you killed a rattlesnake with a crutch."

"I was slap out of shovels. I had to make due."

He cast a glance at the window. "We need to get you somewhere safe, at least for tonight. And we've got to get the window fixed."

"I'll call Handy Andy in the morning. I'm sure he can have the glass changed by the time I get home from work." The brakes came out of last week's check, the window this week. Someone was making it awfully hard to get ahead.

"And tonight?"

"I'll call Lexi."

When she returned to the living room five minutes later, she had toiletries and clothes for tomorrow and the promise of a bed for tonight. Shane opened the front door. But instead of stepping outside he turned to face her. "You sure you're going to be all right?"

"Eventually. I might have a few nightmares first." She forced a smile.

He lifted a hand to cup her cheek. "It's gone. And I'm not going to let anyone hurt you."

His eyes locked with hers, their warm, golden flecks trapped in twin pools of deep hazel. She could easily imagine herself drowning in the concern there. Now would be a good time for that kiss she was thinking about earlier. Anything to pull her thoughts from creepy crawly things.

But not tonight. And not Shane. His gaze dipped to her mouth, lingering for only a second. Then he drew in a deep breath and turned away.

"Let's get you to Lexi's."

Shane sat on the padded stool and swiveled back and forth. Large, glossy books bearing names like *McCall's* and *Simplicity* lay lined up on the sloped counter. A pang of nostalgia shot through him. He was no stranger to fabric stores. Or pattern books. At least the costume section. When he was a kid, his mom practically lived there. Likely still did. His childhood was as far removed from Jess's as it could be. His detective father embodied the title *hero,* and his mom was a good old-fashioned homemaker, a throwback from the June Cleaver era.

He turned to cast another glance at Jess. She was making progress. She might get out of there before Easter after all, in spite of her overly ambitious last-minute customer. It was Carolyn what's-her-name. And she was preparing to clothe half the town of Harmony Grove. At least that's what the healthy stack of fabric bolts seemed to indicate.

When he arrived at six, she'd looked as if she was just getting started. Now, twenty minutes later, she seemed to be winding down. Six bolts of fabric lay stacked on the counter, along with coordinating thread and lengths of cut lace. Jess had already cast several apologetic glances his way. He didn't mind waiting. But the sun had set some time ago, and the western horizon that had blazed red-orange when he first arrived was rapidly turning to navy blue.

When Jess had the final piece of fabric cut and folded, she carried the stack to the register, rang it up and walked Carolyn to the door.

"I'm so sorry," she said once Carolyn was out of earshot. "She came in right before you got here and had a whole list of things she was looking for. At least, a whole list of ideas. It took her another twenty minutes to translate those ideas into specific pieces of fabric."

"Yeah, I noticed."

She strode toward the register and pulled the cash from the drawer. "Fortunately I had everything tallied up before she came in. So I'll just drop this in the safe and close up."

With a swift stroke, she shut the register drawer and headed for the back of the store, platform boots clicking on the vinyl-tile floor. How she stood in those things all day, he'd never understand. But it was hard to imagine her without them. And the well-fitting jeans and the jet black bob. That was her style—chic with a healthy dose of sassy.

He rose from the stool and watched her make her way back up the center aisle. He would see her safely home then walk across the street to his empty apartment and watch TV. Or read. Or maybe even write. He needed to distance himself from her, at least emotionally, before he did something stupid. Like kiss her.

Last night he had come so close. Twice. The relaxed, intimate dinner by candlelight had shattered his defenses and awakened a longing so intense it was almost painful. Then seeing her so vulnerable and terrified had almost finished him off.

He stifled a smile at the image of her beating that snake senseless with the padded top of a crutch. Jess was a bundle of contradictions, which just made her all the more fascinating. She was tougher than most men he had met, but let that silly little dog capture her heart almost from the start. She would confront an intruder in her house or a masked man in the park without a moment's hesitation, but a three-pound snake set her teetering on the edge of hysteria.

"Okay, that's it." She hit the bank of light switches and pushed open the front door. "I've been manning the place almost by myself the past couple of days. BethAnn went into labor. It stopped, and they've got her on semi bed rest, hoping she'll go full-term."

"I hope it all goes well for her." He waited while she locked up, then fell into step beside her and took her hand. Strolling down the sidewalk hand in hand had become a regular routine, but he had refrained from the occasional moonlight kiss.

"How about you? Still employed?" Hope shone from her dark eyes.

"Nope. When I was clocking out, Hammy said I had been replaced, and not to come back on Monday."

Her shoulders fell. "I know we were expecting it, but I still kept hoping they were going to decide to keep you. You didn't happen to stick around and do any snooping, did you?"

"Actually I did. I hoped to get a look at this Nick Lombardi."

"And did you?"

"Nope. Most of the factory was deserted. I guess everyone clears out fast on a Friday afternoon. Everyone except Spike."

"Uh-oh. I think I know where this is going."

Yeah, and it wasn't good. "I went back to the hall where I had overheard the conversation between Spike and Nick earlier. I figured I'd try both of those doors." But not until after checking to make sure no one still occupied the production area at the end of the hall.

"And were they locked?"

"They were." But he had come prepared. He had been halfway through picking the lock when the door at the end of the hall opened. He straightened and slipped the pick and tension wrench into his jacket pocket.

"And that's when Spike came up?"

"Yep. And he wasn't happy to see me hanging around."

"What did you say?"

"I told him I was headed to manufacturing to say bye to Donald, one of the guys who finishes the figurines." Good thing he paid attention to name tags.

"Did he believe you?"

"I don't think so." In fact, he *knew* so. After Spike's gaze dipped several times to Shane's hands still hidden in his pockets, it settled on his face, dark, cold and lethal. Then came the threat. *You and your little girlfriend are gonna learn to quit being so nosy.* Something told him Spike would enjoy teaching that lesson. As long as it didn't put Jess in danger, Spike could bring it on. Angry, defensive criminals tended to make stupid mistakes.

"At least your week at Driggers wasn't a lost cause. We've made the connection between Spike and the guy who kidnapped Lexi."

And he learned his way around. From the factory to shipping and receiving to the offices, he knew the layout of the place, something that would likely come in handy. He was no longer a Driggers employee. But he could probably learn a lot late at night, while the handful of workers on-site were occupied with their "special projects." Sometime this weekend, in the wee hours of the morning after Jess was fast asleep, he would test that theory.

"Well, maybe the FBI can locate him." She looked up at him, hopeful. "You've got someone working on that?"

"I do. I'm sure Nick Lombardi's name is being run through the system as we speak." He smiled down at her in the soft glow of a street lamp. Night had completely fallen, and a full moon hung low in a star-filled sky. It was a beautiful evening, peaceful, clear and a comfortable seventy degrees. Perfect for a romantic walk.

Except someone wanted Jess dead. At least gone from Harmony Grove. And that same someone likely wasn't too fond of *him,* either. He cast an uneasy glance around. A light flashed in the distance, a single dot of red.

Like a laser sight on a rifle or pistol.

Panic ripped through him. In one frantic motion, he grabbed Jess and dived into the hedge along the sidewalk. The simultaneous *psssh* sent a blade of cold terror slicing through him. A second later, he landed on the ground with a thud, Jess's scream echoing in his ears.

She rolled away from him, clutching her shoulder, eyes wide and fear-filled. Denial circled through his mind. *No, not again. It can't be happening again.*

"Jess, what is it? Did I hurt you?" *Dear God, please let that be all.*

She stared at him for several moments, then slowly lowered her hand. A dark stain marked her white sweater, its jagged edge ever expanding.

No, no, no. He shook his head, trying to hold the memories at bay, but they surged forward anyway. Blood roared through his ears, then drained, leaving behind a hollow ring. She had been hit. A bullet meant for him. He scooped her up and sat back on his heels, holding her against him, eyes squeezed shut against the images playing across his imagination.

Sweet, gentle Angie. She was innocent. *He* was the one they were after, the cop who wouldn't give up until justice was done, the adversary who had finally won. It should be *him* lying there, sprawled in the parking lot, face contorted in pain. Instead, he was the one holding *her,* hand pressed to her chest as her lifeblood ebbed through his fingers.

God, no, please don't take her from me.

A moan slid up his throat, ending in muttered words of anguish that made little sense.

"Shane…Shane."

The smooth, low voice cut through his torment, an anchor to the present.

"Shane, I'm all right."

He opened his eyes and drew in a jagged breath. He was in Harmony Grove, kneeling in the grass holding Jess. And she was all right. Relief flooded him, wave after wave, washing away the tension that contracted his muscles and soothing his wild thoughts. His mouth sought hers and he kissed her, hard and deep. She responded beneath him, willing, eager, sharing of herself while drinking in all he had to give.

Then reality intruded like a bolt of lightning. *What am I doing?*

He loosened his grip and eased her back onto the grass. "I'm sorry. I didn't mean… I'm not…"

He snapped his mouth shut and tried to gather his thoughts. "I'm not myself."

"I'm all right. It's just a flesh wound." She didn't reference the kiss, which was a good thing. Talking about it would have made it worse. Wincing, she struggled to a seated position, then again pressed a palm to her shoulder. "We'd better get out of here before they take another shot."

"Of course." He sucked in a fortifying breath, trying to get a grip. What was he thinking, kissing her like that? And where was his head right from the start? All the training? All his years of experience? Some cop he was. A woman under his protection gets shot, and he loses it.

He pulled out his phone. "We've got to get you away from here and to a hospital."

She nodded, but didn't try to rise. Her eyes were beginning to glaze over, and her face didn't hold much more color than her sweater did. He wouldn't try to move her. The shooter had probably taken off immediately on firing the shot. If he had really wanted to kill one of them, he would have fired again. But just in case, his own weapon was in a holster under his jacket. If he got the chance to draw it.

As soon as he disconnected the call, she shook her head. "I didn't even hear anything."

"The gun had a silencer." He sat next to her and pulled her against his side. She was shivering, probably going into shock.

She swiveled her head to look at him. "What did you mean *not again?*"

He had said that out loud? Probably that and more. He had no idea what all had come out of his mouth.

She didn't wait for him to answer. "That was how she died, wasn't it? She was shot."

He could feel her eyes on him but didn't meet her gaze. He couldn't. "Yes," he whispered, "my wife, Angela. She was shot. She died in my arms."

A siren started up nearby, piercing the early-evening silence. The police would arrive in moments.

"How can you still go to church and read the Bible like you do after all that's happened?"

He finally met her gaze. "You're wondering why I'm not angry at God? That's a good question." He let his arm fall from her shoulders and leaned back on his hands. "A lot of times people let circumstances keep them away from God. But it's during the tough times that we need Him the most. When my wife was killed, I was devastated. Again and again I asked God why. But I don't think I was ever really angry. Not at God anyway."

"How could you *not* be angry?"

"God didn't take her from me."

"But He allowed her to be taken. He could have stopped it and didn't."

He drew in a deep breath. "We live in a fallen world, so we're going to have heartaches. But God walks us through them. He gives peace in the storm, strength when we think we can't make it another day."

He pushed himself to his feet. The siren had grown louder, and red and blue strobe lights reflected off their surroundings from somewhere just out of sight. He held out a hand, ready to help her up. "You know, Jess, you don't have to be alone anymore."

She didn't respond, just stared off in the distance, absorbing everything he had said. If only she would believe it. If only she would open her heart to the God he knew.

Finally, she drew in a deep breath and put her hand in his. He helped her to her feet and began moving toward the road where the police cruiser now waited.

But the look of contemplation never left her face.

ELEVEN

Slivers of breaking day sifted through the slats in the miniblinds, and Jessica raised both hands skyward. Stabbing pain stopped her midstretch, and the events of the prior evening tumbled back on her, bringing instant awareness to her sleep-laced brain.

She had been shot. And Shane had held her and kissed her. All along, she had known it wasn't her he was holding. He was stuck somewhere in the past, holding a memory.

And she had kissed him back, partly because she didn't know what else to do, but mostly because it was what she wanted, more than anything in the world. Even if she was borrowing another woman's kisses.

She stretched once more and threw back the covers. She didn't have to get up for work. Shane had seen to that last night, calling BethAnn from the hospital to let her know what had happened. BethAnn had insisted she take the day off, that she would call in some temporary help. At least that was Shane's story.

But Buttons wasn't giving her the luxury of laziness. The instant Jessica moved, Buttons knew she was awake. So he kept nuzzling her arm. When she still didn't respond, a wet tongue slurped up her cheek.

"Oh, yuck." She sat up, wiping her face with the edge of the sheet. Slobbery kisses. That was one thing she would never get used to.

She slipped her feet into her fuzzy slippers and grabbed the leash on the way to the kitchen. Hopefully Buttons would make it quick. She needed a strong cup of coffee. That was nothing unusual—she always needed coffee to wake up. But today she needed it bad.

She hadn't slept well at all. Her preferred sleeping position was curled on her side, alternating between her right and left. The right was fine. But several times during the night, she tried to roll onto her left, and the pain brought her instantly awake.

When she wasn't fighting with sleeping positions, she was plagued by dreams of a faceless menace waiting in the shadows, ready to strike. The fear that had gripped her when the searing pain shot through her shoulder seized her anew with each dream.

She opened the sliding glass door, then touched the bulky square bandage. The doctors said she was lucky. Shane said God was watching out for her. Wherever credit was due, she was thankful. What she had gotten was a little deeper than a flesh wound—the bullet had ripped through some muscle fibers. But at least the bones were untouched.

Jessica looked around as Buttons sniffed yet another bush, hunting for whatever marks a location the perfect potty spot. "Come on, Buttons, go already."

Instead, he circled around the side of the house and headed toward the front yard. Her gaze roamed to Yesteryear Antiques and the apartment above it. Shane would still be inside, probably just beginning to stir also.

Warmth filled her, and an uncharacteristic softness nudged its way into her heart. She was used to taking care of herself. But she had felt so protected lying in the grass, Shane shielding her with his own body. Then he followed her to the emergency room and, once they allowed him to go back, never left her side until she was home and locked safely inside.

She sighed and dropped her gaze to her new charge. He looked as if he was finally getting serious. Yep, this bush just passed the test. In another few minutes, she would be back inside, life-saving brew percolating away.

"Good boy." As she turned to go back, her gaze passed over the driveway and the two cars waiting there side by side. Hers had something on the windshield, tucked under a wiper blade. She crossed the yard, Buttons trotting along beside her, eager for a walk.

"No walk till after morning coffee."

She reached for the envelope, trapped by the wiper blade, and a chill passed over her. She drew her hand back, then chided herself. It wasn't necessarily something bad. Just because someone shot at her...

No, she wasn't taking a chance. She strode back into the house and picked up her phone. She wouldn't tell Shane. He was already pressuring her to leave Harmony Grove and stay out of harm's way. Instead, she called Alan's cell, bypassing Branch altogether.

By the time she had traded PJs for jeans and a sweater and put the coffee on to brew, Alan had arrived. He had the patrol car, which meant he was on duty. At least she didn't drag him away from any personal activities. Although, knowing Alan, he wouldn't have minded.

He jumped from the patrol car wearing a crisp blue uniform and a worried frown. "Are you all right? I heard about what happened last night."

"I think so. But I might have something to add." She pointed at the envelope wedged against the windshield of the Bug.

Alan frowned and walked to his trunk, then came back moments later wearing latex gloves. "I'm glad you didn't touch it. I might be able to lift some prints."

She watched him take the envelope and carefully remove a single page. It was a note, short and to the point, "The first shot was a warning. The next one will be for keeps."

A blanket of dread fell over her, wrapping her in its dark embrace. When her eyes met Alan's, her fear was reflected in his gaze.

"This guy is serious. Hopefully I can get some prints." He dropped the paper and envelope into a zippered bag. "I haven't had any luck so far, but I'm going to keep trying."

"Thanks." She was happy to have Alan in her corner, especially since Branch so clearly wasn't.

Across the street, Shane made his way down the stairs, two at a time. Nothing draws concerned neighbors like a police car in the driveway. She shot him a smile and raised a hand in greeting.

He waved but didn't return the smile. Deep furrows marked the space between his brows, and his mouth was taut with worry. His gaze swept her from head to toe, then settled on her eyes, his own searching. "What's going on?"

"Someone left me a nice little note. Last night was a warning. The next time will be for keeps. Unfortunately, he didn't sign it."

"So now are you convinced you need to leave?" There was a tic in his jaw and a hardness in his eyes that she hadn't noticed before. He would be a formidable foe.

Well, she had enough stubbornness for both of

them. She crossed her arms in front of her. "I'm not turning my back on Prissy." After all the injustice Prissy had endured during her short life, she at least deserved that.

"You can't do her any good if you're dead." He stepped closer to put a hand on her good shoulder. He stared down at her, eyes pleading, and whispered, "Let me catch this guy. I can do this a lot more safely than you can. Remember, I'm trained."

She dropped her gaze so she wouldn't be swayed by those pleading green eyes. His hand on her shoulder was warm, helping to chase away a chill that had nothing to do with the mild morning. She leaned into that warmth, bathing herself in the care and protection Shane seemed to always spread around her. Unfortunately, it was only temporary. Like everything else in her life.

She drew in a deep breath. "I'll think about it."

What he asked of her was almost tempting. Her opponent wasn't fighting fair. Hand to hand, she had a chance. But it was hard to guard against shots speeding silently through the darkness.

As Alan got into his car, another squad car crept past, emblazoned with the words Chief of Police. Shane saw it, too. His gaze followed it up Main Street then returned to her face.

"What are you doing today?"

"I don't know. I was supposed to work and haven't had time to make new plans." The thought of spending the day at home left her with a boulder in her stomach.

"Good. I'll be back in thirty minutes. With plans."

As she watched him walk down the driveway toward the street, some of the heaviness lifted, and a smile crept up her face. That was Shane. Considerate as always. He knew she needed a reprieve. And he was going to make it happen.

Her relief was short-lived. As soon as Shane disappeared, Branch crept back up the road and eased to a stop behind her Bug. He climbed from the car with a series of grunts, then approached with the rolling, cocky gait of someone who thought way too much of himself.

Inside, Buttons went nuts. He bounced between standing at the window, paws on the sill, and scratching at the front door, all the while barking like a crazy thing. He didn't much care for Branch. She didn't much blame him.

Branch stopped at the edge of her porch. "Was my officer just here on police business?"

"He was."

"If that's true, why didn't you go through the usual channels?"

She tried to match his look of disdain. "You know that thorough investigating I was talking about earlier? I was looking for some of that, so I decided to call Alan directly."

For several moments, he stared her down. But

she didn't flinch. Finally, the corners of his mouth arced upward in a menacing leer.

"You know, missy, in case you've forgotten, I can make things pretty difficult for you."

No, she hadn't forgotten. The memory would last well into her golden years. After she and Jasmine toilet-papered Branch's yard, they spent two months in juvie for breaking in to and entering a residence neither of them had ever been inside, and another two months in community service to work off the cost of a watch neither of them had ever seen. Yes, Branch could make her life miserable.

But even Branch wasn't going to stop her from doing what she had vowed to do.

"Aren't you needed somewhere? I mean, I'm sure you have more important things to do than threaten the law-abiding citizens of Harmony Grove."

"I don't know. You're pretty high on my list, missy. And don't you forget it." His threat hung heavy in the air as he spun and sauntered back to his car.

She shook off the uneasiness that had engulfed her the moment he pulled into her drive. With Branch gone, even Buttons seemed to have settled down. Frenzied barking had tapered to an occasional woof. And inside was that long-awaited cup of hot coffee. Life couldn't be all bad.

When the bell rang thirty minutes later, it was Shane who stood on her front porch. Anticipation coursed through her. He had promised to come back with plans. Whatever he had come up with, it would beat staying home alone.

"So where are we going?"

"Honeymoon Island. Do you like the beach?"

"I love the beach."

"Great. We'll hang out, and then I'll take you to my favorite seafood restaurant over there. If you like seafood, that is."

"Mmm, love it. So how do you know about Honeymoon Island?"

"A year or so ago, I was assigned to a case in Clearwater. Whenever I felt as if I needed a break, I'd drive up there and chill." He squatted down and rested on one knee to ruffle the fur on the sides of Buttons's head. "You, my friend, are going to have fun at Mrs. Silverton's today."

Buttons gave a confirming woof and an affectionate slurp up one cheek. Unlike Branch, Shane had gained Buttons's approval from day one and was rewarded with a sloppy kiss each visit. He didn't seem to mind.

He straightened and gave her a broad smile. "It's all set up. I've even packed a picnic lunch. And if you haven't had breakfast yet, I'll swing past a drive-through on the way."

"It sounds as if you've thought of everything."

"I tried." He squeezed her shoulder, his gaze warm. "I want this day to be stress-free."

The concern in his eyes slipped right past every barrier she had erected. It wrapped around her, a welcome blanket of comfort, and she resisted the urge to close her eyes and sink into his embrace. She had no business leaning on someone like that. All too soon, he would be gone and she would once again be alone.

But today, she wouldn't think about that. She would live in the moment and leave all of her problems in Harmony Grove. For the next ten hours, life would be perfect—no money worries, no stress, no killers on the loose.

And a future that included Shane.

While she was pretending, she may as well go all out.

Waves lapped against the shore, a soothing backdrop to the raucous calls of the seagulls swarming overhead. Shane watched Jess tear another bite-size chunk from her leftover dinner roll and toss it into the air. White-and-gray bodies dived, one lucky contender scooping up the morsel.

He smiled over at her. "You know, now that you've brought out the food, you've issued an open invitation to every seagull within a twenty-mile radius. In another sixty seconds it's going to look like a scene from *Revenge of the Birds*."

She grinned back at him, tossed the last piece into the air and brushed off her hands. "They'll lose interest in us pretty fast once they realize the food is gone."

As they ambled farther down the beach, the

swarming cloud above them thinned out. Within a few minutes, all that remained were a couple of lingering hopefuls. The smarter birds had gone off in search of more promising prospects.

Jess drew in a deep breath and released it in a contented sigh. "This has been great. I don't want to go home."

"Me, neither." That was why he had suggested that they drive back over the Dunedin Causeway after dinner and catch the sunset.

He took her hand, entwining her fingers in his. And it wasn't for show. Aside from a few other couples walking hand in hand, there was no one there to observe. Actually, he had taken her hand several times that day as they had walked along the beach, just because he had wanted to. And because it had felt right.

The trip was supposed to be all about Jess, giving her a reprieve, getting her away from the stress in Harmony Grove. But the experience had been as healing for him as it had been for her. There was something about the beach—the sun-warmed sand under his bare feet, the wind on his face, the waves crashing nearby. The cleansing ocean breeze seemed to wash right through him, eroding away the protective shell he had placed around his heart.

Now that Jess knew his past, a barrier had come down, allowing him to connect with her in a way he hadn't experienced in three long years. Now all his reasons for shunning relationships and remaining alone no longer seemed as solid as they had just a couple days ago. The thought terrified him. That sense of determination gave him something to hang on to, a noble strength to take pride in, an unwavering plan for his future. Those resolutions had become so much a part of him that without them, he would flounder.

Jess led him away from the surf and sank onto the sand, pulling him down with her before releasing his hand. A short distance away, waves roared closer, then fell away, advancing and retreating in the unending rhythm of the sea. He crossed his legs at the ankles and leaned back on his hands, the sand soft and cool beneath his palms. When he glanced over at Jess, her eyes were fixed on the western sky, that sunset they had come back for. It was worth the trip. The dazzling display stretched across the horizon, God's own masterpiece painted in broad strokes of orange and pink and lavender.

When Jess finally broke the silence, it was with another contented sigh. "This has been awesome. Thanks for letting me escape for the day. We need to do this again sometime."

"I second that. I'd say we need to make it a regular event."

She flashed him a quirky grin. "That doesn't sound like Mr. Never-Stay-In-One-Place-For-Long. Are you thinking of turning over a new leaf?"

"You never know." The flippant words came easily. So did the shrug that accompanied them. But the nonchalant air was a facade. If he did decide to drop the creed he had lived by for the past three years, it would only happen after some serious soul-searching. And fervent prayer.

And he would do that contemplation alone. Because sitting next to Jess, listening to that smooth, low voice and smelling her fresh scent was not conducive to rational thinking.

He corralled his thoughts and turned to smile at her. "How about you? How long are you staying?"

"I haven't decided. Who knows? Maybe I'll end up moving back. I mean, I don't have anything to go home to. No job. No apartment, as of the end of this month. At least in Harmony Grove, I have a source of income and a place to stay."

And a killer after her. But he planned to remedy that.

She studied him for several moments, her expression thoughtful. "You know, I think you *are* angry with God. Just a little."

He cocked a brow at her. Where had that come from? "Why do you say that?"

"The way you avoid commitment. I think it's a sign that you haven't let things go as well as you think you have."

"So now you're psychoanalyzing me?"

"It's a hobby of mine."

"You're not very good at it." In fact, she was lousy. He wasn't angry at God. Never had been.

She threw back her head and laughed. "Then I

guess I'll have to keep practicing. I'm still trying to figure you out. When I get any more insights, I'll let you know."

He poked her in the ribs then grew serious. The sun had dropped below the horizon some time ago and the colors had faded, leaving only a narrow band of burnt orange stretched across the horizon. Over the next several minutes, the sky deepened from blue to indigo to black until the final remnants of daylight disappeared from view.

Jess drew up her knees, hugging them to her chest. Now that darkness had fallen, the breeze coming off the Gulf carried a damp chill. She was dressed in a T-shirt and denim capris, perfect for the seventy-six-degree high. With the temperature starting to drop and without the warmth of the sun, she could probably use the light jacket she had left in his car.

He stood and held out a hand. "About ready to head back?"

She put her hand in his and allowed him to help her to her feet. "Not really, but I suppose we should relieve Mrs. Silverton of her dog-sitting duties. A lot of older people go to bed early then get up with the chickens."

"Not Mrs. Silverton. She said she won't be going to bed until after the eleven o'clock news. So we've got plenty of time. My guess is we'll be back before ten." Even with the slow, easy amble back to where they had parked.

Jess nodded. "So what are you doing tomorrow?"

"Church in the morning. You're welcome to come. Services are at ten."

"I don't think I'd fit in."

He cast a sideways glance at her. It almost sounded as if she was considering it, hoping for a little nudge to push her over the edge.

"Why not?"

"They all know my past."

"And I'm guessing you know theirs. Or maybe you're the only one in Harmony Grove who has ever messed up. Maybe everyone else is perfect."

She emitted a snort. "Not by a long shot."

"So you'd be right at home."

"I'm not making any promises. I'll give you a definite maybe."

"That's better than a no."

The wind picked up, and a shudder shook her shoulders. He released her hand to pull her against his side and kept her there all the way back to his SUV.

His earlier time estimate proved to be accurate. It was a quarter till ten when he stopped in her driveway. Twenty minutes later, Buttons had been picked up, taken for a potty run and was in for the night.

He turned to face her in the living room. "Are you going to be okay alone tonight?"

She gave him a smile, but it seemed forced. "I'm not alone. I've got Buttons."

"Nothing against Buttons, but I'm afraid he'd lick an intruder to death."

"I don't know. He went nuts when Branch stopped by this morning. If Buttons could have gotten to him, I think he'd have taken a good-size bite."

"Maybe he's a better judge of character than I thought." He moved toward the front door, then stopped. "I could sleep on your couch if you wanted me to, or in the spare bedroom."

"I'll be fine. I've got Prissy's gun."

"And you know how to use it?"

She lifted her shoulders in a prolonged shrug. "Well…"

"Just what I thought. Let me stay."

"I'll be fine, really." She reached for the knob but didn't open the door. Instead, she wrapped him in an appreciative hug, then stepped back, holding his hands in hers. "Thank you for today. You knew I needed a break, and it was really sweet of you to take me away."

"It was my pleasure." He squeezed her hands, all the while wishing for an excuse to pull her back into his arms. Because every time he held her like that, he felt almost whole, the gaping wound in his heart all but healed. In those moments, he was less than a hairbreadth away from tossing aside his resolutions and acting on what he was sure they both felt.

He released her hands and opened the door. "Call me if you need anything. I don't care if it's nothing more than a bump in the night. I'll be over here in two minutes flat, armed and ready."

He waited until the lock slid before stepping off her porch. Clouds drifted in front of an almost-full moon, and a breeze whispered through the huge oak that shadowed a good portion of her front yard. Since Jess refused to leave Harmony Grove, he was going to have to protect her the best he could. Which meant finding Prissy's killer ASAP. Because until every last one of those involved was locked up, Jess was an easy target.

He started toward his vehicle, then stopped to watch headlights move up Main Street. At almost ten-thirty, Harmony Grove resembled a ghost town. Darkened shops sat silent and still in the glow of street lamps, and the houses didn't show much more life than the stores did.

He stepped behind the oak tree and watched the car pass. It was a police cruiser, Branch at the wheel. Was he out patrolling? Alan or Tommy, maybe. But not Branch. He would be hunkered down inside the station. If he even worked a night shift. Shane doubted it. Branch probably left graveyard shifts to one of his subordinates. Unless something was up.

He hurried to his SUV, climbed into the seat and jammed the key into the ignition. By the time he backed from the driveway, Branch had just turned right, heading away from Harmony Grove. What business did he have out there? South of town was a big stretch of nothing, broken by sporadic residences, cow pastures and orange groves.

And one well-known porcelain factory.

Shane held back, unwilling to rouse suspicion. Branch was headed to Driggers. He was sure of it.

When the police cruiser turned off, instead of following, Shane drove past and stopped at the edge of the road to backtrack at a jog. A long asphalt drive led toward the huge brick building. Trees lined both sides, and he hugged their edge. The clouds that had obscured the moon most of the evening parted, casting the landscape in a silver glow, and he moved deeper into the shadows.

The main parking lot held a half dozen vehicles, Branch's cruiser among them. Shane slipped between cars and cast another glance at the sky. Soon he would have cloud cover. Not total darkness, but it would help.

When the moon was somewhat obscured, he dashed toward the building. He wouldn't go in without backup. But he needed evidence. At least reasonable suspicion. Once he had that, he would involve the Bureau.

He slipped along the side of the building, staying in the shadow of the overhang where lack of shrubbery allowed it. The lights from the parking lot didn't reach there, and the chances of someone happening onto him were slim. There was no sidewalk, just a stretch of lawn disappearing into the tree line some twenty feet away.

A burst of light suddenly shone through a window ahead, followed by muffled male voices. He closed the distance at a jog, then flattened himself against the wall. If he wasn't too far off on his calculations, this was the room that always stayed locked.

He cocked his ear toward the window, straining to make out the words. One of the men was Spike, and judging from the tone of voice, he wasn't happy. "Look, this is *my* business, so how about letting me handle it the way I see fit."

"It's your business, but I'm invested in it." That slow Southern drawl belonged to Branch. "No drastic moves unless I say so. You just keep being profitable, and I'll make sure the girl stays out of your way."

"I don't just want her out of my way. I want her gone."

"That's the problem with you." It was the same condescending tone he often used with Jess. "You don't think things through. You're like a loose cannon." Branch moved away as he spoke, the words fading.

Shane turned to chance a peek through the window. Both men had their backs to him. Branch opened the door and stepped into the hall, and Spike left behind him, hitting the switch on his way out.

The room fell into darkness. But he had already gotten a good look. It was a decent size, about fifteen by twenty feet. Boxes stood stacked against two walls, twenty or twenty-five of them. They looked like the same ones he had loaded onto pallets during his brief employment there. But these boxes probably didn't hold figurines.

If only there was a way to know for sure. He couldn't risk calling in the FBI to raid Driggers Porcelain, only to find a bunch of vases and figurines. A mistake like that, and he would blow any chance he had of linking the Driggers boys to Priscilla's murder. But he had to do something.

The more time that passed, the greater the danger to Jess. Maybe they were bluffing, trying to scare her into leaving. But he couldn't count on it. He had to find Prissy's killers. Jess wouldn't be safe until he did. And ensuring her safety trumped everything he was sent to do.

The conversation he overheard raised more questions than it answered. What did Branch mean he was invested in the business? The porcelain business? Or something else?

And who was the girl? A difficult employee? Not likely. No matter how invested Branch was in the porcelain business, he wouldn't stop Spike from firing a problem employee.

No, "the girl" wasn't an employee. It was Jess. She was the one continually getting in the way and refusing to leave.

And for some reason, Branch didn't want her dead.

TWELVE

The gong of the church bell filled the morning air as the sun climbed higher in a cloudless sky. A barely there breeze whispered through the trees, adding to the relaxed ambiance that seemed to have settled over Harmony Grove. It was a perfect morning. Almost.

Jessica drew to a stop and leaned against the light pole at the edge of the sidewalk. Across the street, well-dressed people filed into the redbrick building topped by a white steeple. Shane would be inside, along with BethAnn and her husband. If Jessica could work up the courage, she would join them.

She would never have guessed that coming back to Harmony Grove would lead to any kind of search for God. But Friday night had changed things. It wasn't just the fact that someone had tried to kill her. It was Shane.

Their conversation had been cut short by Branch's arrival. But it had haunted her ever since. Shane's relationship with God was the real deal. She couldn't argue with the peace he had found, couldn't deny that what he believed had given his life meaning. All day at the beach, she wrestled with it off and on. Then last night, he had invited her again. And as she lay in the darkness, Buttons against her side, she made her decision. She was going to see what it was all about.

She pushed herself away from the pole and stepped into the road, her pulse picking up pace in time with her gait. These were people she had known all her life. And they knew *her*. Too well.

Carolyn Platt saw her first and did a double take. So did Lexi Simmons. And she hadn't even made it to the front steps. She drew in a fortifying breath. This was hard enough without having to face the shocked expressions of half the population of Harmony Grove.

As soon as she stepped inside, Roger Tandy met her. His shock was at least mixed with pleasure. The smile he gave her warmed his eyes, and he shook her right hand, slipping a folded sheet of paper into the other. An angry red scar marred his left temple, the only evidence of his run-in with the intruder. Unfortunately, the creep had never been caught.

Jessica stepped away from Roger to move farther into the building, and her eyes dipped to what she held. It was some kind of program for the service. Hopefully she wouldn't need it. Shane would guide her and keep her from making a fool of herself. If she could find him.

She scanned those seated, searching for a familiar sandy blond head. When she found it, her stomach clenched. *Third row from the front?* She would rather slide inconspicuously into the back. But parading all the way up the center aisle was more desirable than sitting alone.

She sucked in a deep breath and made her way forward as six people stepped onto the platform. Three took positions at microphones and the other three at instruments. She watched a familiar figure settle onto the stool behind the drum set, and her jaw went slack. *Jarrod Wilson?* He had run with Hammy all through junior and senior high and had gotten in almost as much trouble. Now he was playing for church? Maybe there was hope for her yet.

When she reached the third row, Shane turned to welcome her. The warm smile that crept up his face created a momentary flutter in her stomach. She tamped it down with a casual smile of her own.

"I decided to check it out."

"That's great." He stood so she could slide in next to BethAnn. Maybe he thought she would be more comfortable sandwiched between two friends. Or less able to make a quick getaway.

The small band on the platform broke into song, and as if on cue, those in the audience stood to their feet and began to clap in time to the music. She stole a glance at Shane then at some of the others around them. This wasn't the starchy, somber atmosphere she had pictured.

202 Motive for Murder

Actually, she didn't have anything pictured. It wasn't that she had never been inside a church building before, because she had. But weddings and funerals didn't count. Neither did sneaking into the social hall during services and loosening the lids on the salt shakers.

The band segued into the next song, and her gaze settled on Jarrod. He played with an enthusiasm that was contagious, eyes shining with excitement above an ever-present smile. Maybe she could talk to him later. If he still had anything to do with Hammy, he might be able to tell her something.

As soon as the service ended, Shane smiled over at her. "So what did you think?"

"It was pretty good." The music was fun, the sermon engaging. But there was something there she couldn't grasp, something that seemed to reach most of the worshipers without quite touching her. It radiated from those on the platform, and when she stole a glance at Shane, then BethAnn, it was there, too. These people weren't worshiping a distant, uncaring God. They were experiencing Him in a way she never had.

She followed Shane into the aisle. "I'd like to speak with the drummer. He and Hammy were pretty good friends at one point. He might know something."

Disappointment settled in his eyes.

She flashed him a teasing smile. "Don't worry. I paid attention. I wasn't in investigative mode the whole time. Come on." She invited him along with a wave of her hand.

When she reached the front, Jarrod was just stepping down from the platform. Jarrod was still Jarrod. The same relaxed shuffle. The same mischievous glint in his eyes. And the same shaggy brown hair that reached his shoulders. But something had changed. And it was more than just maturity. He seemed grounded. More at peace.

"Wow, Jess! It's good to see you."

The friendly greeting was expected. The hug wasn't. By the time she recovered enough to hug him back, he had already released her.

"I haven't seen you around," she said. "I thought you had left Harmony Grove."

"Sort of. I moved to Lakeland to be closer to my job. It was either make that thirty-minute trip five times a week for work or twice a week for church."

She motioned toward Shane. "This is my friend, Shane Dalton."

Jarrod shook his hand. "Jessica and I go way back. Similar history. We were both voted least likely to be caught dead inside a church."

Jessica laughed, but his statement wasn't far from the truth. "Something must have changed for you, and somehow I don't think it's the money."

"No, they don't pay me for this. I do it because I want to. I finally got my life straightened out. Or I should say God straightened me out. I didn't have much to do with it."

He started down the aisle, and Jessica fell in beside him. Since his life revolved around church and clean living, Hammy probably wasn't a part of it anymore. But it was worth a shot.

"Do you still hang out with Hammy?"

"No, I'm afraid not. He says I'm no fun anymore. He hasn't figured out that life's actually more fun without drinking, smoking weed and getting into trouble. But I keep working on him. Hey, if God can get a hold of me and you, He can get a hold of Hammy, right?"

She stole a glance at Shane. She wasn't exactly in the God-got-a-hold-of-me camp. But standing next to Shane, she didn't feel like a total outsider. She shifted her gaze back to Jarrod. "Have you talked to him since my sister died?"

"Yeah, once. I don't know how much of the visit he remembers. He was pretty drunk."

Yeah, he was apparently that way a lot lately. She glanced around at the people filing out the door with them and lowered her voice. "Did he tell you anything about how she died?"

"He said she OD'd on oxycodone. Really sad."

She nodded, then studied him for several moments. Could she trust him? Did she have a choice? If Hammy was going to open up to anyone, it would be Jarrod, his one-time best friend.

"Can I level with you, without it going any further?"

He answered without hesitation. "Sure."

She led him into the churchyard, away from the other members clustered in small groups. Shane followed, jaw set beneath a warning glance that was hard to ignore. He was about to be very unhappy with her. But they were nowhere near finding out who killed Prissy. And she wasn't about to pass up a good lead.

"We have reason to believe Prissy was murdered."

Jarrod's eyes widened. "You don't think Hammy did it, do you?"

"No, but we think he knows who did. He won't talk to me, but maybe he'll talk to you."

"I don't know." Jarrod shifted his weight from one foot to the other. "At one time, maybe. But we haven't been close for the last two years."

He shifted his weight again, features set in indecision. He probably didn't want to get involved. She didn't blame him. But she needed his help.

"I know my sister and I had our issues, but Prissy didn't deserve this. If she was murdered, I really want to find her killer. Will you help me?"

Jarrod drew in a deep breath, then gave a sharp nod. "I'll go talk to him this afternoon and see what I can find out. If I learn anything, I'll call you."

Shane cleared his throat, and she shifted her gaze to his face. The warning glance had morphed into a worried scowl. She gave Jarrod her cell number and watched him program it into his phone. "Please don't tell him you talked to me."

"No problem."

BethAnn approached as Jarrod dropped the phone back into its pouch. "I invited Shane to dinner, but there's always room for one more. Can you come?"

"I've got to run home and let Buttons out, but I can be there in twenty minutes."

BethAnn and Kevin headed toward their car, but Shane stayed. The rigid jaw and hard gaze underlined the scowl already there. "I'll walk with you."

His tone didn't give her an option. They had barely made it to the sidewalk when he started. "You just made a big mistake." His voice was taut. "Even if he doesn't mention your name, Hammy and Spike are going to know it was you."

"They already know I'm asking questions. That's nothing new."

"And the more you push, the more danger you put yourself in." The tension radiating off of him seeped into her pores, and she tried to shrug it off. She didn't need his reminder. She was well aware of the danger. But she refused to turn her back on Prissy again.

She jammed her key into the front-door lock. "I'm careful. And I've got Prissy's gun."

"That might be some consolation if you knew how to use it."

"Then I'll learn." She pushed open the door. "Look, I've been taking care of myself for almost my whole life. So you need to back off."

He followed her inside. "And you need to stop

selfishly charging ahead without any consideration for how your actions affect the people around you."

Her jaw dropped, and she spun to face him. *Selfish?* He was calling her selfish? Everything she was doing, she was doing for Prissy, trying to make up for all the things she didn't do when she had the chance.

The indignant retort never made it to her lips. His gaze softened, and he gently traced her jawline with the back of one index finger.

"There are people who care about you, Jess."

Yeah, that was what he kept saying. She was just having a hard time believing it. When they were kids, Priscilla fought for the attention she craved by being sweet and compliant. Jessica just walked around with a Texas-size chip on her shoulder, telling herself she didn't need anyone's love or attention, all the while hoping someone would care enough to try to prove her wrong. No one ever did.

"Why? Why are you so concerned about me?"

"Because I care." He tilted her face up to meet his. "You're a special lady, Jess, and don't ever let anyone tell you otherwise."

She stared up at him, her gaze captured by warm green eyes that seemed to look right into her soul. He had a knack for knowing what she needed to hear and just the way to say it. He told her she was special. At the moment, she believed it. He made her *feel* special. And cherished. And complete.

But he was leaving. Not today or tomorrow or even next week. But eventually he would be gone.

She lifted both hands to cup his strong jaw. "When are you going to stop running? When will you put the past to rest and grab hold of the future?" She searched his eyes, watching the battle that raged in their depths—the longing to take the risk and open his heart, facing off with the voice of caution.

And she sought to soothe the pain of his memories in the only way she knew. She slid her arms around his neck, stretching to her tiptoes while she pulled him closer. Her lips met his, and for several moments, he didn't move. Then his arms encircled her waist, and the tension seemed to drain from his body. What she initiated, he took over, leading in a way that was urgent and demanding.

And she had no doubt. He wasn't trapped in some distant memory. He was kissing *her*.

Completely and fully.

A bulging half moon hung suspended in a cloudless sky, stars sprinkled across the endless expanse. Beneath, the world lay quiet and still, the silence broken only by the occasional hoot of an owl. Shane strolled up the sidewalk, watching for a familiar set of headlights. He had already circled Jess's house three times, scanning the shadowed landscape for any threats. But the Parker property was as still as the rest of Harmony Grove.

Up ahead, a street light cast its soft glow, and he

stopped to look at his watch. A quarter till eleven. It wasn't *that* late. But Jess out alone after dark was cause for concern no matter what time it was. *Lord, please bring her home safely.*

Several hours earlier, while she was at work, he called a couple of gun clubs in Lakeland and enrolled her in a four-hour intro-to-handguns course. The class ended at ten, and the drive home was a full thirty minutes. If she stayed after, even for a short time, it would easily be eleven o'clock by the time she got home. So a quarter till was far too early to start worrying.

But he wouldn't rest easy until he saw those familiar round headlights moving up Main Street. He should have gone with her. He could have read while he waited, or hit the mall or something. Instead, he had spent the past thirty minutes alternating between praying and pacing.

He had completely lost his objectivity. Forget objectivity—he had lost his professionalism. There were guidelines for interacting with people involved in cases. Posing as boyfriend and girlfriend for investigation purposes was one thing. Kissing her like he had yesterday was entirely another, regardless of who initiated it.

The problem was, he was falling in love with her and had no idea what to do about it.

A car turned onto Main Street a half mile up the road, and anticipation surged through him. Definitely Volkswagen headlights. It drew closer, slowed and turned into the Parker driveway. He met her at the door before she could get out.

"So how did it go?"

"All right. It's not as easy as it looks." She reached across the car to pick up the thirty-eight lying on the seat beside her. His own weapon was hidden under his jacket. "I know more than I did this morning, but if I'm going to be expected to actually hit something, I'll need some more practice. I seem to do better with a well-placed kick."

"Yeah, I think I remember that."

She stepped from the car and walked toward the house. Other than briefly telling her about the class, he hadn't spoken to her all day.

"Anything exciting happen today?"

"Not really, but I did learn that Driggers Porcelain was broken into Saturday night."

"Really?"

"Yep. I know it's true, 'cause I got it straight from Carolyn Platt." She flashed him a goofy grin.

"Without a doubt. So did they take anything?"

"A couple boxes of vases, some really expensive ones." She unlocked the door and let them inside. He wouldn't stay long, but he wanted to know the latest. Ever since her conversation with Jarrod yesterday, he had been on edge. Jarrod didn't seem the type to rat her out. At least not intentionally. But things could slip.

Jessica dropped her purse on the end table and laid the weapon beside it. "Driggers' thief wasn't very smart, though. According to Carolyn, he left fingerprints all over the place."

"That's interesting. I thought the Driggers boys were the ones behind all the mischief in Harmony Grove. But since it was their place that was burglarized, I'd say we have a suspect we haven't even considered."

Was he a simple burglar, out to make a quick buck by pawning some vases? Or was the theft a smoke screen to throw the authorities off his real purpose? Was he looking for something? If so, was it the same thing Prissy had stumbled on?

Jessica nodded. "Hopefully they'll get a match on the prints."

He moved toward the door, then gave her a totally appropriate peck on the cheek. Her day was over. His was just beginning. Enrolling Jess in a gun course wasn't the only thing he had accomplished while she was at work. He had had a long talk with Ross, who shared his frustration. The case had dragged on far too long. Almost three months with no real breaks. And since coming to Harmony Grove and getting wrapped up in the Parker matter, the stakes had gotten much higher. They already had one body, with a killer thinking of making it two.

As much as he would like to set up a raid on Driggers Porcelain, if he jumped the gun and acted too soon, he would jeopardize the whole operation. He needed some solid evidence. So far, he had lots of hunches—overheard conversations, vague references that may or may not have anything to do with the Parker girl or his drug case. And he had the photo. The third man was still unidentified. But Ross said they were working on it.

What he really needed to do was get inside Driggers Porcelain and find out what was in those boxes. His gut told him it wasn't figurines. If his hunch proved right, maybe they would find evidence linking the Driggers brothers to both cases. And bring Branch down in the process.

So tonight, during that two-or three-hour span of time between the night shift leaving the factory and the regular employees showing up for work in the morning, he would do some investigating of his own. Unofficially, of course.

Shane jogged up the stairs to his apartment, energy spiking through him. Hopefully by morning, he would have good news for Jess.

Shane waited in the shadows. Sounds of the woods surrounding him. The hoot of an owl rode on a gentle breeze, punctuating the crickets' monotonous song. Some small creature nosed about nearby, probably an armadillo or possum.

The special projects crew was working extra late tonight. Light emanated from several of the factory's windows, and since he had arrived almost two hours ago, no one had even come out for a smoke break. The crew of six moved about inside, supervised by Spike. But Shane couldn't see what they were doing, even with the binoculars that hung from a strap around his neck.

Light filled a darkened room, the same one he had viewed Saturday night. He lifted the binoculars and watched as eight boxes were brought in and stacked. Then the room fell into darkness, and one by one, each of the other windows went black. Moments later, voices broke the stillness of the night as the men filed from the building and into the parking lot at its rear. Shane moved closer, staying inside the tree line.

Spike was the last to leave. He turned and locked the door behind him. "Thanks for the extra effort. You'll be well compensated."

After the last vehicle circled the building to make its way up the asphalt drive, Shane waited several more minutes, then stole through the darkness to the back door. His lock-picking tools were in one jacket pocket, his flashlight in another. He set to work on the lock, keeping a constant eye out for any sign of approaching headlights.

Several minutes later, he breathed a prayer for protection and success and slipped quietly inside. There was no alarm. The fact that someone had broken in the previous night was proof. Besides, during his brief employment, he had checked. None of the doors or windows were equipped with sensors. Spike probably didn't see the necessity of a security system in a place like Harmony Grove. After last night, though, he might rethink it.

Shane relocked the door behind him and pulled the flashlight from his pocket. If anyone came back, the rattle of a key in the lock would give him warning. He probably should have a lookout. But he didn't trust the local police. There was no question Branch was dirty. But unless he had totally lost his ability to size people up, Alan didn't have a dishonest bone in his body. And Tommy Patterson, while a decade or two older, seemed to fly as straight as Alan. But he wasn't staking his life on his impressions of people he had known for three weeks.

And he wasn't ready to involve the Bureau. Tonight he was acting on his own, breaking and entering without a warrant. Jess's time was running out. Branch sounded as if he didn't plan to kill her, but whatever he had in mind for getting her out of the way couldn't be good.

Shane clicked on the flashlight and started down the hall. He knew where he was going and what he was looking for. If all went well, he would be in and out in thirty minutes and have all the evidence he needed.

He stopped at the locked door and once again set to work. The inside lock was easier to pick, and in a few minutes he was in. He eyed the boxes stacked three high, covering two walls and part of a third. There was something important in those boxes, something incriminating enough to kill for.

He slid one of the boxes from the stack and placed it on the floor. A single piece of clear packing tape sealed the top. He pulled a pocketknife from his jeans pocket and dropped to his knees. If he needed to hide his actions, he would get some tape from the warehouse and carefully place it over what he had cut. No one would notice unless they were looking for it.

His heart pounded as he opened the flaps to reveal...*figurines?*

No, there had to be more in this locked room than figurines. He removed two of them from the box. They weren't even anything special. A brown-skinned worker wearing blue jeans, a colorful plaid shirt and a sombrero gripped the handle of a rake. The craftsmanship was okay, but not spectacular. Driggers produced pieces for every budget. These were from one of the lower end lines, not like the vases Jess told him had been stolen.

He repacked the two figurines and tried another box. It held the same sombrero-topped figures the other one had. He removed several of them, searching the rest of the box, but except for the figurines and their packaging, it was empty.

Maybe the top boxes were decoys. Maybe the real treasure was beneath. He moved to the other side of the room and laid several boxes out on the floor, exposing the lower ones. Then he cut into a third. It too held figurines, this time a salsa dancer.

Surely Prissy wasn't killed over some figurines,

no matter how exotic. Whatever the Driggers brothers were into, it wasn't in this room. He rose from the floor and, using the flashlight to guide him, made his way to the warehouse. When he got back to the room, he would check a couple more boxes, then tape them all up and restack everything the way it was. Finding what he was looking for may take more than one night. In the meantime, he wasn't going to tip anyone off.

He searched the rest of the building by flashlight and came up empty-handed. In another hour, warehouse employees would begin to arrive. He needed to be long gone before that first car pulled into the parking lot.

He heaved a weary sigh and trudged toward the back door. His covert activities didn't bring him any nearer to solving either case—the drug running or Prissy's murder. Maybe the Driggers brothers weren't connected with his drug case. But they had their hands in something other than manufacturing porcelain. And Priscilla Parker had stumbled onto what that was.

It was there, somewhere in the building.

He was just missing it.

THIRTEEN

Jessica slid her lunch into the fridge in the back room at BethAnn's. Shane had just said goodbye outside, with a promise to return shortly before six. Now that he was once again unemployed, he was back to walking her to work and taking Buttons out at lunchtime.

There hadn't been any repeat of Sunday's passionate kiss. Between work and her class Monday night, there hadn't been time. And yesterday, a temp filled in at BethAnn's while she made a quick run to Miami to put her things in storage. Fortunately, the apartment was furnished, and she wasn't a pack rat like her sister.

But with Shane, all the time in the world wouldn't have made a difference. She had hoped Sunday's kiss was a turning point. It wasn't. He hadn't withdrawn, but he seemed reserved, tentative, like a child afraid of the water, dipping in a toe, then a foot. That was okay. She had no business jumping into anything herself.

The bell on the front door jangled, and she straightened and closed the refrigerator. A customer already? It wasn't even nine o'clock.

She stepped from the back room as BethAnn walked into the store. Or maybe *walked* wasn't a good word for it. Fewer than two weeks from her due date, she was solidly in the waddle stage.

"I thought you had a doctor's appointment this morning."

"I thought I did, too, but it's not till tomorrow. They say you lose a few brain cells with each pregnancy. I think it's starting already." She grinned and slipped her purse into a drawer under the counter. She would probably stay for a couple of hours then go back home to rest. "So how did your class go last night?"

"It was fun. I don't think I'll ever be a sharp-shooter, but I did put a hurting on that paper guy I was shooting at. I figure since I inherited a gun, I might as well learn how to use it."

She hadn't told BethAnn her real reasons for enrolling in the class. BethAnn didn't seem like the type that appreciated a lot of drama. And Jessica wasn't about to do anything that would jeopardize her job. Besides the fact that she needed to eat, she liked working at BethAnn's.

BethAnn shook her head. "I'm still having a hard time picturing Priscilla handling a gun. She was always so…prissy." She grinned. "No pun intended."

BethAnn was right. Prissy wouldn't have gotten a gun unless she felt she needed it.

Jessica closed the register drawer and arranged the latest sale flyers. "The credit card machine's almost out of paper. I ought to change it while you're here, just in case there's a trick to it. From the looks of things, I'll be on my own any day now."

"I certainly hope so. I'm so ready for this munchkin to get here. But not earlier than he should."

BethAnn disappeared into the storage closet at the back, and Jessica began to stock the register drawer with change. Across the street, two police cars eased to a stop, the oft-seen chief-mobile with the shared cruiser right behind it. Branch's blue and red lights reflected in the windows of the surrounding shops. Whoever brought up the rear evidently decided to pass on the light show.

Jessica stopped what she was doing to watch. Something was going on, something important enough to require the services of two thirds of the Harmony Grove Police Department. Branch swung open the car door and struggled to his feet, adjusting his belt over his girth as he straightened. His right hand hid an object. He used his left to motion impatiently to the other driver, unidentifiable through the tinted windows.

The door swung open, and Alan climbed from the car. He hesitated for several moments, then moved toward Branch with angry steps, his mouth set in a firm line.

Whatever was bothering him, it didn't touch Branch. He was smiling, a devious, scheming grin that set her nerves on edge. He started across Main Street, adjusting his grip on whatever he held, and a metal object dropped, swinging from a short chain. A handcuff.

A sick feeling of dread slid down her throat, lining her stomach with lead. Why was Branch walking toward BethAnn's carrying handcuffs?

He swung open the door and motioned Alan inside. When Alan stepped over the threshold, there wasn't even a hint of the ready smile he always had for her, and the gaze he settled on her was dark and brooding. But there was something else, too. Regret. An unspoken apology.

Branch marched boldly into the store as Beth-Ann came out of the back holding a twelve-pack of receipt tape. He stood a few feet in front of the counter, posture set in his usual self-important stance—weight shifted to his heels, hands on his hips, chest out and chin raised.

BethAnn laid the tape on the counter and addressed him. "Can I help you?"

"You can help most by staying out of the way."

BethAnn raised her brows. She probably hadn't seen the condescending side of Branch. "Since you're standing in my store, how about telling me what the problem is."

"I'll be glad to." He gave Jess a smile, but there was nothing friendly about it. When he turned back to BethAnn, the smile was still there. "It seems you've hired a criminal."

Jessica tried to still her racing pulse. "You're lying. You know full well I haven't done anything."

"The evidence says otherwise."

"What evidence?"

"Why don't you tell her, Alan?"

Alan's jaw muscles twitched as he clenched his teeth. Barely restrained fury flowed just beneath the controlled exterior. Alan was all about justice, something she wouldn't get on Branch's watch. Alan drew in a deep breath. "You know the break-in that happened at Driggers Porcelain a couple nights ago? Chief says it was your prints they found."

Her heart was pounding in earnest now, and her ears began to ring. "He's lying. I've never been inside the place." Surely Alan didn't believe him.

Branch shook his head. "Sorry, missy, the evidence doesn't lie."

"No, but dirty cops do. Whatever evidence you have, you planted it, and you're not going to get away with it."

He made a clucking sound, still shaking his head, then lifted the handcuffs toward Alan. "Go ahead and cuff her and read her her rights."

A sick sense of déjà vu engulfed her. She was being framed again, set up to pay for a crime she didn't commit. But this time it would follow her for the rest of her life.

Panic spiraled through her. She was on a runaway train, hurling through the darkness toward her own destruction. "I'm going to talk," she said, grasping at anything that might halt the chain of events. "You've been threatening me since I came back, trying to run me off. Well, it's going to back-fire on you."

Branch crossed his arms in front of him, resting them comfortably on his belly. "And who do you think they'll believe, an upstanding citizen like my-self, with almost forty years of public service, or someone with your history?"

"That was all juvenile stuff."

"Not *all* of it."

So Branch knew about the trouble she had got-ten into when she first moved to Miami. He had checked her out.

He nodded toward Alan. "Go ahead, son. Being a good cop sometimes involves bringing to justice the people we consider friends. But we have to up-hold the law no matter what."

She would have snorted in disgust if she wasn't so terrified. Branch didn't uphold the law. He rode above it.

Alan took the cuffs, the tenseness in his jaw be-coming a visible tic. But a softness had entered his blue eyes. He *did* believe her. Not that it would do her any good. Branch was in charge, and he had "evidence."

Alan secured the cuffs on her wrists. "You have the right to remain silent. Anything you say or do may be used against you in a court of law." A determination she had never seen before replaced the softness in his gaze. He finished the notice, then dropped his voice to the merest hint of a whisper. "Hang loose. I'm working on it."

She drew in a deep breath and tried to corral her scattered thoughts. What did Alan mean, he was working on it? Freeing her? Bringing down Branch? Maybe both? She wasn't holding out very high hopes. Branch was right. No one was going to believe her word against his. He had told her if she stayed, she'd be sorry. He had made good on his threats.

She cast a glance at BethAnn, but couldn't read what was behind those green eyes. Did BethAnn believe Branch? Did she have any reason not to?

"Okay, let's go." Branch's words jarred her from her thoughts and sent another round of panic ricocheting through her. She was going to jail. As an adult.

Branch reached for her arm, but she twisted away and moved toward the door before he could touch her. Just before stepping outside, she tossed desperate words over her shoulder. "Please get a hold of Shane and tell him what's happened."

Maybe there was something he could do. She didn't expect him to bail her out. And she didn't want him to. She had no way to pay him back, and she wasn't about to become beholden to anyone. But maybe he could use his position to pull strings.

She stepped outside into the midmorning sun. It was another beautiful winter day in Florida. But she had a hard time appreciating it. All she had wanted was to find Prissy's killer. But she wouldn't be much good to anybody locked up.

She headed toward the car Alan and Tommy shared, staying a step or two ahead of Branch. He wasn't going to touch her, if she had anything to say about it. He clamped a hand around her forearm anyway and directed her toward his car. She jerked from his grasp. Of course he wouldn't let her ride with Alan. He didn't want her talking to him.

Branch opened the back door, and she ducked into the seat, unable to avoid the pushy nudge against her shoulder. He couldn't resist that last show of control. Someday someone would bring him down. She only hoped she would be there to see it.

For the next twenty minutes, she rode looking through the mesh-filled glass in front of her. Unfortunately, it was a familiar experience. As they neared Bartow, her pulse picked up again. The county jail was fewer than three miles away. Soon she would be going through processing, being fingerprinted, having a mug shot taken and trading her chic sweater, jeans and boots for the nondescript uniform the inmates wore.

She squared her shoulders and summoned some optimism. Branch had won this round. But she wasn't defeated. It would take more than a stint in jail to bring her to her knees. She was a fighter. And if any of her fellow inmates thought they could intimidate the new kid on the block, they would find out really quickly how wrong they were.

Branch eased to a stop next to the three-story stucco building, and her heart jumped to double time. Who was she kidding? The tough pep talk wouldn't do anything to change the truth.

She had just landed in a world of trouble.

And she was scared to death.

"We've got a match on the guy in the photo."

Shane gripped the phone more tightly at Ross's words, excitement spiking through him. "Yes?"

"Juan Moreno. He works for Colombian drug lord Santiago Zapata."

"Bingo." That was the link connecting the Driggers brothers to the downed plane. And very possibly what the Parker girl had stumbled onto.

"You think you can get solid enough evidence for us to set up a raid?"

"I don't know. If it's at the factory, I'm missing it." He sank onto the couch. "Everything there seems to be on the up-and-up. Even with the night crew. There's nothing at Driggers Porcelain except porcelain."

"Maybe you and the team should stake it out, see who's coming and going, especially at night."

Ross was right. Whatever criminal dealings Hammy and Spike were involved in, the factory was a logical place to meet, even if the drugs never made it inside. Especially with an airstrip right out back. He hadn't seen or heard any small planes fly over. But if they approached from the south, their flight would end five miles before they reached Harmony Grove.

"I'll work on it, see what I—" A knock on the door interrupted his thought, seven sharp raps filled with impatience. Or maybe he was injecting the urgency into what he heard, due to his own frustration. He ended the call with Ross and rose from the couch.

The raps came again, more insistent than the first time. Yep, someone was definitely impatient.

He tucked his weapon into the waistband of his pants, letting his shirt drape over it. With no peephole in the door and no windows that offered a view of the stairs, he wasn't taking any chances.

When he swung open the door, BethAnn stood there wringing her hands. His stomach did a freefall, crashing to a stop near his knees. Something had happened to Jess.

"What's going on?"

"Jessica has been arrested."

"What?" The word exploded from his mouth.

"Branch and Alan came into the store and took her away in handcuffs. Said the prints left at Driggers the other night were hers."

He stepped away from the door and started to pace. "I knew something was going to happen, but I didn't expect this."

BethAnn moved inside and closed the door. "What do you mean?"

"Branch has been trying to get her to leave ever since she got here. When simple coercion didn't work, he resorted to threats. Priscilla Parker didn't commit suicide. She was murdered. And the closer Jess gets to the truth, the more Branch wants her out of the way."

BethAnn stood in silence for several moments, letting his words sink in. Jess obviously hadn't shared the details with her. "Is there anything I can do? I mean, I'd be happy to be a character reference for her. She's been nothing but upright and honest during the three weeks she's worked at the store."

"We'll see. It may not come to that."

"Well," BethAnn said, reaching for the door, "I need to get back to the store. I just closed everything up and came right here."

He shut the door and snatched his cell phone from the coffee table. He would pull some strings. And if he couldn't manage that, he would use his own money to pay bail. His actions were against his better judgment. Because until he got the case solved, the county jail was the safest place for her to be.

But if he left her there, she would never forgive him. And that would be more than he could bear.

Shane sat in the small lobby area of the Polk County Jail, ankle crossed over one knee, fingers entwined in his lap. The distinctive click of heels against the vinyl-tile floor drew his attention to the door leading from the lobby into the jail. A second later, it swung open, and Jess stepped through. She didn't look any worse for the wear after her day in the pen. Actually, she looked quite good. Her makeup wasn't even smudged, proof that she had accepted her fate without tears. Somehow that didn't surprise him. It was hard to picture Jess dissolving into tears about anything.

He held the door for her then followed her out into the late afternoon shadows. She didn't look as happy to see him as he had expected.

"They told me I'm free to go but didn't tell me how. I hope you didn't bail me out, because I don't have the money to repay you."

So that was what was bothering her. "Don't worry. You don't owe me anything."

She cast him a sideways glance. "Did you post bond?"

"I did, but it was minimal." It would have taken a little more time to get the charges dropped. It also may have gotten back to Branch and blown his cover.

"Then I *do* owe you." She crossed her arms in front of her. "I didn't want you to bail me out."

"Come on, Jess, let me do something nice for you. You can't go your whole life not accepting help from anyone."

He clicked the key fob, and the accompanying beep signaled that the vehicle was unlocked. But

Jess didn't get in, even after he opened the door for her. She uncrossed her arms to plant her hands on her hips.

"I've taken care of myself since I was eighteen. From the moment I walked out of that shelter and put money down on a dumpy little apartment, I've paid my own bills. I don't want to be obligated to anyone."

"Even me?"

She studied him for several moments, back ramrod straight. "Especially you."

What did she mean by that? He probably didn't want to know.

"If you insist, you can repay me when you get back on your feet."

"By that point, you'll be long gone, and I don't want to have to hunt you down to repay you. I believe in clean breaks." She brushed past him and began walking toward the road that ran alongside the jail.

He hurried to catch up with her. "Are you saying once I finish my case here you never want to see me again?"

"That's right."

Her words sliced right through him. "Why?"

When she reached the sidewalk, she turned away from Broadway, the main road, and kept walking. "Because I know your type, guys who don't stick around. From the time I was three years old, that's all men have done, walked in then back out of my life."

"What if I'm different? What if I don't *want* to walk out of your life?"

She skidded to a stop and turned to face him, her dark eyes searching his. Cautious hope swam in their depths, buried beneath layers of betrayal. "What are you saying?"

His heart constricted, the longing inside tangling with fear. Because no matter how careful he was, how attentive and diligent, there was always the possibility it could happen again. Over the course of almost a decade of law enforcement, he had made enemies. One could strike at any time. He had already lost one love. Was he willing to risk another? Could he do that to Jess? Could he do it to himself?

He shook his head. "I don't know."

Her shoulders sank, and she turned to walk back to his vehicle.

He fell in behind her, the weight of regret bending his own shoulders. He had hurt her. But he had no choice. Because he truly didn't know.

And he would never make a promise that he might not be able to keep.

FOURTEEN

Jessica sat with her elbow against the door, chin in her hand, watching but not really seeing the landscape fly past the passenger window.

"Jess, I'm sorry. I just—"

She turned and held up a hand to stop him. "It's all right. You don't need to explain."

She couldn't be upset with him. He had made it clear right from the start—he wasn't the type to settle down. But she fell for him anyway.

Several more moments passed in silence. Then Shane turned to her again. "Am I taking you home or to BethAnn's?"

"Take me to BethAnn's." It was only five o'clock, an hour till closing. She probably no longer had a job. But it was worth a try.

He cast a tentative glance her way. "Can I still walk you home?"

"Of course. We're still working together, at least for the time being." She forced a smile. "We'll even keep up the pretense for the residents of Harmony Grove."

There was no reason not to. After all, nothing had changed, at least on his end. On hers, she had just given herself a dose of realism. Nurturing impossible dreams was a waste of time. No matter how strong the attraction, no matter how intimately they connected, Shane would never let himself love again.

"I really wish you'd pull back and just let me handle everything." He cast her a worried frown. "Branch is determined to get you out of the way. Since this didn't work, I hate to think about what he might try next."

"I'm not giving up until Prissy's killers are caught." She had voiced the argument before. More than once. But this time her tone lacked conviction. Shane was right. Branch and his buddies weren't likely to give up easily.

Shane pulled into a parking space in front of BethAnn's. "It's not worth the risk. As much as I enjoy working together, I can do this without you."

She started to climb from the vehicle, but Shane's voice stopped her.

"I have your purse. BethAnn brought it to me." He reached behind the seat and lifted it from the floorboard.

"Thanks." She hadn't even thought about it. But when Branch hauled her away that morning, it was still in the back room at BethAnn's. She turned to face him fully. "And thank you for bailing me out. I know I didn't seem very grateful, but I do appreciate it. And I *will* get you paid back, even if I have to make installments."

"Installments are fine, but you don't need to pay me back."

"I know, but I—"

This time *he* held up a hand. "I know, you always pay your bills."

As she watched him pull away from the curb, an acute sense of loss swept over her. He would stay until he wrapped up his case. But she was two small steps away from heading back to Miami as soon as she could get everything wrapped up. If she did, Branch would win. Whatever involvement he had in Prissy's murder would be between him and his Maker.

And once she left, she would never see Shane again. All she would have is a mailing address, a place to send checks until she had him paid off.

She stepped onto the curb and stood for several moments in front of BethAnn's, trying to work up the courage to go in. She wasn't beyond begging. She really needed the money. For her own bills as well as Prissy's. Mark had tried repeatedly to schedule another hearing before Judge Peterson, and each time was told there was nothing available on the docket until April.

So she was on her own. If BethAnn didn't want her back, it didn't look good. No one else was likely to offer her work after Branch had marched her across Main Street in handcuffs, lights flashing.

The only way he could have made it more obvious was if he had used his siren.

After one more moment of hesitation, she squared her shoulders and swung open the door, ready to give it her best shot. Maybe she had half a chance. BethAnn was in a bad spot, ready to burst any day and on semi bed rest. And she would be hard-pressed to get someone else hired and trained quickly enough to completely handle the store alone.

BethAnn glanced up with a ready smile. It faded instantly, and her eyes widened in shock. "Jessica?"

"Shane bailed me out." That was all she was going to tell her. She wouldn't do anything to blow his cover or put his life in danger.

"That's...great. Wow, this is unexpected."

Jessica tried to read her. She seemed hesitant. Was it because she was caught off guard? Or did BethAnn no longer want her in the store?

"I was framed. You can ask Shane. Branch has my prints, but he didn't get them at the factory." Spending the day in jail had given her plenty of time to think. For the charges to stick, Branch would have to have lifted her prints from somewhere. "The day the store was broken into, he spent an awful lot of time dusting. Silly me, I thought he was trying to lift the intruder's prints. Instead he was lifting mine to save for later, just in case."

"Branch went to a lot of trouble to frame you."

Jessica nodded. "He wants me gone. Shane and

I have discovered some things that leave no doubt that Priscilla was murdered."

"Yeah, Shane told me."

Some of the tension fled her shoulders. Shane had prepared the way. So what she had to say wouldn't seem so far-fetched. "Whatever happened, Branch is covering it up. He's been trying to get me to leave ever since I got here. And someone else has, too. My getting shot wasn't just some random act of violence. The next morning, there was a note left on my car letting me know it was a warning, that the next time it'll be for real."

BethAnn's eyes widened again, and she brought a hand to her mouth. "Oh, my."

"I'm sorry I didn't level with you before. I was afraid if you knew everything that was going on, you wouldn't want the drama and would let me go. And I really need this job." She sucked in a deep breath and released it in a long sigh. "But if you want me to leave, I understand."

"No, I don't want you to leave. None of this is your fault."

Relief flooded through her. "Thank you."

"Frankly, I've never liked Branch. He's always seemed kind of…I don't know, shifty. And that's on top of being a conceited blow bag." BethAnn grinned, washing away the last of Jess's concerns.

"That's an understatement." She clapped her hands together. "Well, since I'm still an employee, I guess I'd better get to work. I've got forty-five minutes to get something accomplished. Anything in particular you want me to do?"

"Yeah, I got a couple of orders in this afternoon that I haven't put out yet, some fabric and a box of housewares. How about tagging and putting those items out?"

"Will do." She headed to the storage closet. First the housewares. After some direction from BethAnn on pricing, she set about rearranging the shelves, making room for the new merchandise. The figurines that BethAnn put out three weeks ago were all still there, minus the one that went the first day. "These haven't sold very well."

"They haven't," BethAnn agreed. "Just the one Marge Tandy bought the day I put them out."

Jess's hand stopped in midair as a chill passed through her. "Marge Tandy bought the figurine?" Her heart began to pound, and a fine sheen of perspiration suddenly coated her palms.

BethAnn must have heard something in her voice, because she looked at her sharply. "Yeah. Why?"

"The Tandys' house was broken into the same night the store was. I suspected there was a connection, and that's it. They were after the statues."

BethAnn shook her head, brows drawn together in confusion. "But they didn't take the statues. They didn't take anything."

"No, they didn't *take* the statues. They *switched* them."

"What do you mean?"

"When I came in that morning, the statues had been moved. Not much, but I could tell. I had straightened the shelves before I left the day before. I had those figurines in three neat rows, each facing perfectly forward. But the next morning, the rows were crooked, and all of the figurines had been turned a few degrees one direction or the other. At the time I thought it was odd that someone had moved them all but not taken any."

"What do you think it means?"

"You bought the figurines, and they got them mixed up and delivered the wrong ones."

"But they were identical."

"They *looked* identical. But there had to have been some difference. Enough to break into the store to get the original ones back. And then, when one was missing, they had to find out who bought it."

BethAnn nodded. "That's why they rifled through the receipts."

"Yep. And it led them to the Tandys. The only problem is, they didn't anticipate Roger Tandy getting up during the night and stumbling in on them."

"So what are you going to do?"

The jingling of the bell on the front door saved her from having to respond. Mrs. Silverton ambled into the store and occupied BethAnn's attention for the next several minutes.

Jess went back to stocking and pricing, mulling BethAnn's question over in her mind. She should probably tell Shane what she had learned. She had finally found the link that connected all the random events together.

But what if she was wrong? What if she told Shane, he got his team together to raid Driggers Porcelain and they found nothing? No, she needed to be sure. And if she was right, she would prove her worth.

Tonight she would go to Driggers and see what she could find out. She wouldn't do anything stupid. She would just stay outside and watch from a safe distance. Maybe she would get lucky and stumble on something important. Apparently Prissy had.

According to Carolyn, Hammy bought the Lotus for Prissy. Was that two grand a week another of Hammy's gifts? Or was it payment to buy her silence? And did the Driggers brothers finally get tired of paying out?

It was possible. No, it was more than possible. It was likely.

She had no delusions about who she was dealing with. Given the right circumstances, either of them could be capable of murder, especially Spike.

But there was one big difference between her and her sister. She wasn't greedy or stupid enough to blackmail them.

Shane laid the book aside for the third time and pushed himself to his feet. For how well it was holding his interest, the spy thriller he was reading might just as well have been a college economics textbook.

He crossed the room to stand at the front window, something he had done more times than he could count since walking Jess home at six-fifteen. As always, his gaze drifted to the left, as if pulled by some unseen force. A street lamp cast an amber glow over the sidewalk, and just beyond, the Lotus and Bug sat next to each other, nestled in for the night. He took comfort in the sight. It meant Jess was inside, shades drawn and doors locked.

Within ten minutes of arriving home, she had headed out again, planting a small seed of worry in his gut. For the next hour, that seed sprouted and grew until it commandeered all his thoughts. By the time she pulled back in an hour later and climbed from the car with her bags of groceries, he was a borderline basket case.

Now she was safe. At least as safe as she could be all alone in the house. Her lights had gone off around nine, leaving only the blue glow of the television emanating through the small window in the front door. She was likely already asleep. After all, she had had an exhausting day. Getting arrested. Spending several hours in jail. Facing an insecure future.

He moved away from the window and strolled to the kitchen. He wasn't hungry. He wasn't really tired, either, even though it was almost midnight. He was just restless. He opened the fridge door and stood for several moments, staring inside. Finally, he removed an apple and sank his teeth into its juicy sweetness.

How could he have done it? After all he had been through, everything he had learned, he had totally fallen for Jess. Maybe once this was all over, he would have the fortitude to stick with his vow and walk away.

The problem was, his heart had stopped listening to logic. Jess had managed to weave her way right past all his defenses. And that wasn't a good thing. Those walls around his heart were there for a reason. They protected not only himself, but everyone around him. And he would keep reminding himself of that, no matter how much he yearned for a future that included Jess.

He tossed the apple core into the trash and leaned against the wall. A single lamp burned in the living area, on the table next to the couch. He really should turn it off and go to bed. Instead, he sank onto the couch and picked up the worn leather Bible from the coffee table. Time and again, he had found comfort within those pages.

Jess insisted he was angry at God. She was wrong. He wasn't harboring anger toward God. He would never understand why things happened the way they did, but he wasn't angry. Just the opposite. The tougher things got, the more he depended on God.

He let the Bible fall open three-fourths of the way

to the end. Yellow highlighter drew his eyes to the final verses of Matthew 11.

Come to Me, all you who labor and are heavy laden and I will give you rest. Take My yoke upon you and learn from Me, for I am gentle and lowly in heart, and you will find rest for your souls. For My yoke is easy and My burden is light.

It was one of his favorite passages. He had come back to it again and again over the years. And he was back tonight, seeking rest for his soul.

He drew in a slow, deep breath and closed his eyes, waiting for the peace of God to wash over him. Instead, an image intruded, expressive dark eyes filled with hope, right alongside betrayal.

God, help me to forget about her.

But what if that wasn't what God wanted? What if God wanted to use him to bring her healing? And what if God wanted to use *her* to bring *him* healing? Was he ready?

The resulting flash of insight provided the answer. No, he wasn't ready. Three long years later, he was still burying the pain deep inside where nothing could touch it.

He wasn't angry with God, but he hadn't accepted the healing Christ offered, either. Instead, he had triple-wrapped his heart and boxed it up, unwilling to risk that kind of pain again. It was easy to tell himself he was doing it for those he cared about. But in the stark truth of God's Word and Jess's accusations, he couldn't deny it. Everything he had done during the past three years had been as much to insulate against his own pain as it had been to protect others.

He pushed himself to his feet and started to pace. He didn't know where to begin. Guarding his heart had become a way of life. *God, help me to let go. I'm ready to receive your healing. And if Jess is the one you have chosen for me, please make it work out.*

He stopped pacing and drew in a deep breath. The urge to see her at that moment was overwhelming. But it was late. He couldn't march over there and bang on her door at midnight.

Tomorrow morning, he would tell her how he felt. She had touched him in the deepest way, and he couldn't imagine living his life without her. She was light to his darkness—no matter what happened, she refused to let circumstances get her down and charged ahead with determination and enthusiasm.

He strode toward the window. A hundred yards of night separated them, but as he lifted his hand to the glass, he somehow felt closer to her. Then his gaze fell on her driveway, and panic stabbed through him.

The Bug was gone. It was there just thirty minutes ago.

Anger warred with the anxiety spiraling through

his system. How was he supposed to protect her when she wasn't doing anything to protect herself? What was she thinking, venturing out in the wee hours of the morning?

Maybe she got another middle-of-the-night call. If so, she was supposed to get ahold of him.

He flew down the steps, taking them two at a time, and slid into the driver's seat of his SUV. The last time, the orders were to come to the park. So that was where he went. There were two parking areas, one at each end. Her car wasn't in either of them.

There was only one other possibility. And though it was the most dangerous, it was also the most likely.

He reached the end of Main Street, took a right and sped off into the darkness, all the while praying he was wrong.

FIFTEEN

The sky rumbled and the ground shook as a twin-engine plane descended out of the darkness and touched down on the concrete airstrip. It sailed past with a roar and a whoosh of air, and Jessica cringed. She stood some thirty feet away, hidden just inside the trees that bordered the Driggerses' private runway. Hopefully close enough to learn what she needed to know, but far enough away to eliminate any risk of getting caught.

She had left her car alongside a dirt road a quarter mile past Driggers and hiked back to find the parking lot deserted except for a single black Maserati, which belonged to Spike. If there was a night crew, they had been given the night off. Whatever work there was to do that evening, evidently Hammy and Spike could handle it on their own. They had carried box after box out of the warehouse and stacked them next to the runway.

Now Spike stood with a hand on one hip, weight shifted to that leg, and a cigarette in the other hand.

As he waited for the plane to stop, he took a long drag and slowly released it in a stream of gray smoke that curled upward and dissipated in the light breeze. As usual, he radiated confidence, a dark sense of controlled power. With his black hair slicked back, impeccably fitting silk shirt and tailored suit, success rolled off of him. Not like an owner of a multi-million-dollar business. More like a drug kingpin or a mafia boss.

Hammy didn't possess the same self-assured air. He always came across as trying hard to emulate his smooth older brother but never quite succeeding. At the moment, he stood at the edge of the runway with Spike, hands resting in his pockets in what should have been a relaxed pose. But his stiff posture and the way he fidgeted, shifting his weight from one foot to the other, broadcast his discomfort.

The plane skidded to a stop, and the whine of the props slowly dropped in pitch, then faded to silence, carried away on the late-night breeze. A half moon bathed the scene in a silver glow. The runway lights did even more, offering her a perspective not much inferior to daytime.

The pilot and his passenger emerged from the plane and walked back to where Spike and Hammy waited. The passenger carried a large leather satchel. When he turned, her heart jumped into her throat. He was the third man in the photo. She was about to witness what Prissy had.

She moved a little closer, still staying hidden in

the shadow of the trees. She didn't recognize the pilot. Whoever the figure at the edge of the photo was, it wasn't him. He was too thin.

Spike spoke first. "Twenty cases, like you ordered."

The man handed the satchel to the pilot and approached the stack of boxes. After slicing the tape on one of them, he reached inside and withdrew a figurine.

Jessica watched as he turned it over in his hand, studying it under one of the lights. These weren't ordinary figurines. Hammy and Spike wouldn't show up in the middle of the night to pawn off some common knickknacks. There was something special about them. Just like the ones originally delivered to BethAnn's.

Suddenly he thrust sharply downward, sending the figurine crashing to the concrete, and Jessica flinched. Shattered chips of porcelain lay at his feet, and he bent to retrieve something from the debris. When he straightened, he held a plastic bag filled with white powder.

"One hundred percent pure," Spike said. "As always."

The buyer opened the bag and removed a pinch, manipulating it between his thumb and index finger. Apparently satisfied, he signaled the pilot, who handed the satchel to Spike.

Spike dropped to his knees and lifted the leather flap. Inside was money, lots of it. He pulled out a thick wad of bound bills and fanned through them. After pulling out several more and rifling through the bag, he stood to his feet. "And I can assume it's all here?"

"Of course."

Jessica watched, mind reeling, as they loaded box after box into the plane. She had just witnessed a drug deal go down. And this wasn't your typical sell-to-the-neighborhood-crackheads drug deal. This was huge. She would wait until the plane took off and Hammy and Spike had gone back inside. Then she would leave her hiding place to go home and call Shane. She finally had the evidence he needed to set up a raid.

After the last box was loaded, the pilot and passenger got back into the plane, turned it around and taxied down the runway. Hammy and Spike watched it lift into the air.

"Another successful deal," Spike said. "The Man will be here any minute for his share." He cast a sideways glance at Hammy. "At least those are the only greedy palms touching our money now."

Hammy bristled. "You didn't have to kill her."

"You were letting her blackmail you, dude. That's not too smart."

"That was *my* business."

"It was your business till she came to me for more." Spike turned and walked toward the door going into the warehouse. "Someday, when you're no longer all moon-eyed over her, you're going to thank me for getting rid of her."

"No, I'll never thank you. Someday I might just kill you for it."

Spike laughed off the threat. "You don't have the guts."

Jessica chewed her lower lip. There was someone else coming, which meant instead of making her getaway as soon as Hammy and Spike disappeared inside, she'd better stay put. Trudging through the woods in the middle of the night wasn't an option. Neither was slipping along the edge of the tree line and out to the road, knowing that at any moment she could be cast in the glow of someone's headlights.

Spike reached for the doorknob. Suddenly branches rustled overhead, and she stifled a gasp. Both men turned to look as an owl flew from the pine tree next to her, circled the area over the airstrip, then once again disappeared into the woods.

For several tense moments she waited, willing them to go inside. Then Spike's hand dropped from the doorknob, and he turned to stare into the woods, right at where she stood. There was no way he could see her. But that didn't hold the panic at bay. Or slow the pounding of her heart. Or quell the urge to bolt from her hiding place and run full speed through the woods.

But her safest bet was to stay calm and not make a sound. She slid around the back side of the tree, wishing she had chosen an oak instead of a pine.

Its narrow trunk didn't quite hide her, even if she turned sideways.

Spike stepped onto the airstrip and moved closer. Hopefully he would stop, scan the trees and, hearing nothing, go back inside. Some twenty feet from where she stood, he reached under his jacket with his right hand and pulled out a gun.

Her pulse jumped to double time, but she didn't move. She had the advantage. She could see him better than he could see her. If he got too close, she would use the element of surprise, kick the gun from his grasp and subdue him. Then she would only have Hammy to worry about. But *he* wasn't as likely to shoot her.

Spike took a step closer. His left hand went into his pants pocket, and keys jingled. What was he getting now? A second later, he withdrew his keys, and a skinny beam of sharp white light penetrated the darkness around her.

With her plans shattered in an instant, she bolted from her hiding place to run deeper into the woods. A shot rang out, and bark sprayed from a tree as she passed, each piece like a minimissile, leaving behind a stinging welt.

God, help me! She hadn't tried praying to Shane's God. At least not seriously. And she wasn't even sure if He would listen. But the panicked plea rang through her mind anyway. She ran as fast as she could, stumbling through the darkness as heavy footsteps closed in.

Then her toe caught a root, sending her crashing to the ground. Pain shot through one knee and the opposite wrist. The heavy footsteps stopped, right next to her, and she squeezed her eyes shut against the inevitable.

But instead of a bullet, a rough hand gripped a fistful of her hair and pulled her to her feet. Still holding her by the hair, Spike jerked her head back and shone the light in her face.

"You. I should have known you'd follow in your sister's footsteps."

A stray shaft of moonlight fell across his face. His lips were curled back in a sneer, and his eyes shone with manic pleasure.

A gleam of wicked delight.

Shane ran for all he was worth, right up the middle of Driggers Porcelain's drive, all stealth forgotten. Less than a minute earlier a gunshot had pierced the still night, and he hoped to God it had nothing to do with Jess. *Lord, please let her be all right.*

He hadn't seen her car. But he knew Jess, and she was smart enough to not leave it in plain sight. She was here. He was sure of it.

As he neared the building, he stepped off the asphalt drive to let the grass muffle his footsteps. A faint male voice drifted to him, too far away to pick up the words. Someone was behind the building.

He crept along its side, moving soundlessly toward the back. The voices grew louder and closer. It was Hammy and Spike, and they seemed to be arguing. But there was no female voice.

Maybe Jess wasn't here after all. A glimmer of hope flickered inside. He would check to be sure. Then he would leave. As much as he wanted to see what he could learn by eavesdropping on Hammy and Spike's argument, Jess was still out there somewhere.

He peered around the corner, and his heart almost stopped.

Spike had Jess by the hair, dragging her across the concrete airstrip. His other hand held a gun, cocked and ready to fire. It was pointed at her head.

A cold blade of fear sliced through him. He had been in similar situations before, life-and-death showdowns where one or more people were likely to end up dead.

But this time it was the woman he loved. And that made all the difference in the world.

Heart pounding, he drew his gun and aimed. But he couldn't get a clear shot. From his vantage point, Jess was in front of Spike. Besides, Hammy probably had a gun also. If Shane fired a shot, Hammy would, too, maybe even shoot Jess.

He clenched his fist in frustration. Nothing was going as planned. He had no backup, no one that even knew he was here. His plan had been to find Jess, get her to give up whatever harebrained scheme she had concocted and go back home.

Instead he had found himself outnumbered and outgunned.

Hammy stepped forward and grabbed Spike's arm. "You can't shoot her."

"Wanna make a bet? She knows too much. Just like her sister did."

"You better talk to the Man before you do anything. He's not very happy with you."

Jess tried to turn around, but Spike only tightened his grip on her hair, jerking her head farther backward and twisting her neck into what had to be a painfully awkward position. She winced and dropped to her knees.

"Go ahead and shoot me." Her words sounded strained. "You're both going down. The FBI has had an agent assigned to Harmony Grove for the last month, and they're closing in. So you might as well give up."

If her words shook Spike, he didn't show it. Hammy did.

"See what you've done?" His voice was raised several pitches. "Now the FBI is on our tail."

"She's bluffing, you idiot. The FBI doesn't have anything on us."

Hammy started to back away, hands held up in front of him. "Well, I don't want any part of killing people, man."

"If you're going to go weak on me, maybe I don't

need *you* around, either." Spike aimed his weapon at Hammy's chest.

Hammy shrugged. "Go ahead. I don't care anymore."

Shane watched the exchange with interest. When this was all over, Hammy would probably talk. In fact, getting Hammy to accept a deal to testify against his brother in exchange for his own freedom was a distinct possibility.

Now to figure out how to rescue Jess.

Spike waved the gun toward the door but didn't release her. "Come on. Let's go inside."

As soon as the three of them disappeared into the building, Shane whipped out his cell phone. He couldn't chance calling 911. More than likely Branch would intercept the call. Instead, he pulled up his contacts and selected Alan's cell number.

Alan answered on the third ring, his "Hello" rather slurred.

"Alan, it's Shane. I don't have much time, so get something to write with."

"Shane, what's going on?" All traces of sleep had left his voice, and judging from the scrapes and bumps that came through the phone, he had evidently gotten out of bed. "Is Jessica all right?"

"No, Spike has her, and he's threatening to shoot her." He continued right over the other man's gasp and any questions he might have. "I need you to call this number and tell Mike to get the team together and come to Driggers Porcelain. Then call Tommy and get over here yourselves. But don't go in until my guys get here." He didn't know what Alan and Tommy would be able to do. But it would take his team at least thirty minutes to get there from Lakeland. In the meantime, Alan and Tommy would be in place.

He ended the call, then tried to formulate a game plan. Whatever happened, he couldn't wait for backup to arrive. Jess had gotten a reprieve, but it was only temporary. Eventually the Man would arrive. Hammy and Spike were willing to leave her fate in his hands. Who was he? Someone higher up than Hammy and Spike, someone who was calling all the shots?

Shane tried the door that Hammy and Spike had just entered. It was unlocked. But he couldn't open it and march in without knowing where they were. He started to circle the building, doubling back the way he had come, looking in windows and listening for muffled voices. There were none, and although several lights were on, the rooms were empty.

When he reached the locked room with all the boxes, it looked bare compared to what he had seen just two nights ago. At least half of the boxes had disappeared. What was left lined one wall and part of a second. What had happened to the other boxes in so short a time?

He started to turn away from the window, and the ice cold barrel of a pistol pressed into his neck, freezing him. The familiar click of metal on metal told him the gun was cocked and ready to fire.

"Well, well, well."

It was Branch. What was he doing there? Did he have Alan's phone bugged? No, he couldn't have gotten there that fast.

"Spike warned me we might have company. You and your nosy little lady just had to get involved, didn't you?"

So he had talked to Spike. But as quickly as he had gotten there, he must have already been on his way out. But why? Why would Branch be meeting Hammy and Spike at the factory in the middle of the night? They must have had prearranged business. Maybe Branch was the Man.

The barrel of the gun pressed harder into his neck. "Come on, hands in the air. We're going inside."

Shane slowly lifted his hands, heart pounding in his chest. His own weapon was under his jacket, within easy reach. But any sudden moves would likely get him killed. Branch was out of shape, but Shane had no doubt that he could still fire a gun.

Shane turned and began walking toward the back door, movements slow and fluid. He wouldn't do anything to startle Branch. Within moments, he would be inside, with Jess. Then he could decide on a course of action.

Judging from Hammy's comment, the Man would decide their fates. If the Man was Branch, it didn't look good. Branch would do whatever he had to to keep his criminal activities secret.

The metal door clicked shut behind them, an ominous tone of finality that sent hopelessness washing over him. He drew in a fortifying breath. His men were on the way. Alan and Tommy would be there any minute. Maybe they were already there, slipping silently through the woods. If he could just stall for thirty minutes.

God, please get them here fast.

SIXTEEN

Jessica drifted on the edge of consciousness, floating on a sea of pain. There was no sense of time or place, just this terrible pounding in her head, a keen-edged agony the strength of twenty migraines.

She tried to move, and a wave of nausea swept through her. A moan climbed up her throat, escaping through her nose.

Where was she, and why did she hurt so badly?

She swallowed hard. Something was covering her mouth. Her eyes snapped open, and memory came rushing back to her like a boulder rolling down a steep slope.

She was at the factory. Spike had hauled her inside. When he sent Hammy in search of some rope to tie her up, she knew it might be her last chance to escape. A solid kick had sent the gun flying, and another one had knocked him to the floor. She had reached the gun just as a hard fist slammed into her temple. And that was the last thing she remembered.

Now she was sitting in a chair in the warehouse,

pallets of boxes all around. Her hands were tied behind her back, and duct tape covered her mouth. She tried to shift her position and found her legs were tied, too.

Nearby, Hammy and Spike stood with their backs to her, each leaning against a pallet. Spike had a phone pressed to his ear. He lowered it and swiped a finger across its screen. "He's not answering. He should have been here by now."

At the other end of the warehouse, a door slammed shut, and both men straightened. Hope flickered briefly, the thought that maybe Shane had come for her. Then practicality took over. Of course it wasn't Shane. He was home in bed, fast asleep. The same place she should be.

Coming out alone was a stupid idea. Because now the unthinkable had happened. She was gagged and tied to a chair while, twenty feet away, Spike made plans to kill her. And she couldn't blame her predicament on anyone but herself.

And she couldn't count on anyone to help her. Especially not God. She had spent her whole life ignoring Him. Or worse yet, blaming Him for everything bad that had happened to her. Why would He even listen to her?

Maybe because He loves me?

The thought came out of nowhere. She had spent too much time with Shane. He believed God loved everyone, no matter what they had done, and that forgiveness was there for the asking. Surely there had to be more to it than that.

The footsteps grew closer, irregular, as if more than one set. She leaned to the side, trying to see around pallets, and winced as a red-hot streak shot through pain that had calmed to a sickening throb. The angle left her a narrow but clear view between pallets.

Shane! He had come for her.

An unexpected rush of emotion sent tears surging forward. No, she refused to fall apart. She had been through the terror of getting caught, the threat of death and the pain of a blow to the head. Not once had she dissolved into tears. And she wasn't going to do it now, not even tears of relief.

But that relief didn't last long. Shane wasn't alone. Branch walked behind and to the side, and judging from the way Shane held his hands in the air, Branch's weapon was drawn.

"Look what I found outside snooping around." He shoved Shane forward, keeping his gun trained on him.

Spike drew his and doubled the fire power. He nodded toward Hammy. "Tie him up and tape his mouth. And make sure he's not armed. If he resists, I'll shoot the girl."

Branch shook his head and raked first Spike and then Hammy with his disapproving gaze. He had mastered that expression of condescension designed to make everyone else feel small. It didn't matter that both Hammy and Spike were a whole head taller than he was.

"See what a mess you boys have gotten yourselves into? Getting you out of this one might be impossible. Even for me."

Spike turned on Hammy. "If you weren't my little brother, you'd already be at the bottom of Lake Mae wearing custom-made concrete boots."

"Me? You're blaming this mess on me?" Hammy's indignation spilled out in his words. He finished his task, handing Shane's gun to Branch, then straightened to face off with Spike. "If you hadn't killed Priscilla, these two wouldn't be here right now."

"You didn't leave me much choice. You shouldn't have brought her here to begin with."

"Hey, that wasn't my fault. She was with me when you called. You said I needed to get right over here. I told her to stay in the car."

"Well, she obviously didn't listen." Spike moved a step closer to Hammy, gesturing as he spoke. "And then you were dumb enough to pay out money to keep her quiet. If she would have just been satisfied, she'd still be here, with you wrapped around her little finger, and I would have been none the wiser. But she had to get greedy and come to me. Well, I have a lot more effective ways of ensuring someone's silence than paying out my hard-earned money."

"Okay, children," Branch interrupted. "Save your

sibling bickering for when I don't have to listen to it. That's not what I came here for."

Spike turned to Branch, his irritation with his brother seemingly gone in an instant. "No, we know what you came here for." He walked over to the leather satchel and pulled out four wads of bills, which Branch stuffed into both front pants pockets.

"So what do we do with *them?*" Spike inclined his head toward his prisoners.

"I think you *know* the answer to that."

Jess crumpled as a wave of despair washed over her. Until that moment she had harbored some sliver of hope that they would somehow get out of there alive.

God, please protect us. Please send help. I'm not ready to die tonight. The frantic pleas raced through her mind, circling around again and again. She didn't deserve God's help, but Shane did. He had done nothing but live for the God he served, devoting his life to protecting the innocent and bringing the not-so-innocent to justice. In fact, if it weren't for her, he wouldn't even be there.

Before Spike could respond to Branch's words, a loud knock reverberated through the building, coming from the direction of the front door. Hammy and Spike looked at each other with fear-filled eyes. Spike immediately hid his panic, stuffing it behind his usual cool demeanor. Hammy remained wide-eyed and tense, looking as if he was ready to bolt at any moment.

Branch didn't even flinch. Whatever threat was just outside, he probably viewed himself as above it. "Go see who's there."

Hammy ran through the warehouse and returned a half minute later. If anything, his panic was more pronounced. "It's a squad car."

"Harmony Grove?"

"Can't tell. I didn't open the door, just looked through the window. It's parked straight toward the building, so I couldn't see the side."

The banging sounded again, this time more insistent.

"Go," Branch commanded with a sharp wave of his hand. "Tell them everything's under control."

"And if they don't take my word for it and insist on coming in?"

"If it's Alan or Tommy, I'll take care of it."

"And if it's not?" Spike spoke this time. Some of Hammy's fear seemed to have seeped into him.

"Then *you'll* take care of it."

Spike addressed Branch, his tone cold, lethal. "So you're just throwing us to the wolves."

"Hey, if I go to jail, who's going to keep your sorry rears out of trouble?"

Spike studied Branch for several moments, then gave a minuscule nod. Hammy once again disappeared.

And Jessica continued to pray.

* * *

Shane watched Hammy jog away and cast Jess a wary look. His agents couldn't have arrived that quickly. Not more than twenty minutes had passed since he placed the call to Alan. The cruiser sitting outside had to belong to Alan or Tommy.

What were they doing? Shane's instructions had been clear. Alan and Tommy weren't to try to come inside. They were to wait outside until his agents showed up. His men were more qualified than a couple of small-town cops to handle situations like this. If Alan and Tommy charged in trying to be heroes, they chanced getting them all killed.

A tense two minutes later, Hammy returned. He was winded, probably from apprehension as much as the exertion of running the length of the building. He wasn't the seasoned criminal that his brother was. "It's Alan. He's asking about Jessica and Shane. I told him they both ran off into the woods, but he still wants to come in and check."

"I'll handle Alan." Branch turned to follow Hammy, but with none of the urgency that the younger man was showing. Branch seemed to have one speed, an ambling saunter.

When Branch came back into the room, it was at that same relaxed pace.

"Well?" Spike asked, his tone impatient.

Branch shrugged. "He's gone."

Spike's eyes were filled with caution. "Are you sure?"

"Positive. I watched him turn around and go back

up the drive and out to the road." Branch spoke with a confidence that left no doubt. "I told him I've searched the whole place, and there's not a trace of them, so he can go back to bed." His lips curled up in a devious grin. "And my guys always obey their chief."

Spike nodded toward Shane. "This one must have called them before you caught him."

"Yep," Branch agreed. "He underestimates my reach. At least we don't have to worry about any more visits tonight."

Shane smiled behind the tape, and respect for the young officer rose up within. Alan wasn't simply disobeying orders. His knocking on the door was brilliant. Not only would Hammy, Spike and Branch let down their guard, believing that no one else was coming, but his men would know there were three bad guys to take down instead of two. And he had bought them some time.

Spike asked his earlier question again. "So what do we do with these two? How do you want to get rid of them?"

Branch shrugged. "Shoot 'em. Bury 'em in the woods, drop 'em in the lake, whatever. Just don't leave me a mess to deal with this time."

Shane's heart started to pound. They had to stall. All they needed was another five minutes or so, and his men would be in place. *Lord, please let them get here in time.*

Spike raised his brows. "You really want to off an FBI agent?"

"FBI?" Branch looked at Shane sharply, panic in his eyes. But just that quickly, it was gone. "I won't be offing an FBI agent. You will." He crossed his arms and leaned back against one of the pallets. "Untie their legs and take them outside."

The distraction Shane prayed for came then, courtesy of Hammy. Over the past twenty minutes, he had slowly come unhinged. Now the inevitability of being an accomplice in a double murder pushed him over the edge.

He began to shake his head, stepping backward until a pallet stopped him. "No, I can't do this." His voice rose, in both pitch and volume. "I won't be any part of killing someone. We're going to get caught. Someone's going to find out. Then we'll spend the rest of our lives in prison. Maybe even get the chair."

"Shut up!" Spike's words were loud and sharp, penetrating Hammy's hysteria like a red-hot poker cutting through lard. He aimed his weapon at his frazzled little brother. "If you don't get a grip, you'll be joining these two."

Hammy's gaze darted around the room for several moments as he clenched and unclenched his fists. When he seemed to have regained control, Spike lowered his weapon.

"Now get them untied. And watch her feet."

Shane smiled at Spike's caution as a new respect

for Jess welled up inside. Whatever happened, she wouldn't take it lying down. She would fight till her dying breath.

Hammy finished untying their feet and removed the rope that bound each of them to their chairs. Spike lifted the weapon.

"Now get up and walk. And if either of you try anything, I'll shoot you right here."

Shane locked gazes with Jess, trying to send her a silent message. He shook his head no, almost imperceptibly. They needed to make it outside. Help would arrive at any moment.

Jess's eyes communicated a message of their own—apology, sadness, regret for what could have been. And love. He knew it as surely as if she were able to say the words.

They rose from their chairs, but before they could take their first steps, Hammy's voice cut in.

"I'm not going." An unusual strength filled his words, especially in view of his hysteria a few moments ago. "You do what you have to, but I'm not watching."

Spike hesitated for an extended beat, eyes raking Hammy up and down. They held indecision. And disgust. Finally he spoke. "Fine. If you're too much of a wimp to do what needs to be done, just stay inside. I've got enough guts for both of us."

He began to herd them toward the back door, and Shane stepped into the lead, only to set the pace.

Walking slowly could buy them an extra thirty seconds. And in situations like this, every second counted.

Just before they reached the door, Spike ordered them to stop and moved in front of them. He held the door wide. Shane stepped into the mild night, followed by Jess. The airstrip lay ahead, and beyond that, the woods. A light breeze rustled the trees, a steady whisper that would be soothing under any other circumstances.

Alan and Tommy were out there somewhere. He knew that for a fact. Had his own men made it yet? *Lord, please get them here quickly. And please give them wisdom and success.*

He cast another glance at Jess. She walked beside him, staring straight ahead, jaw rigid, chin held high. Stoic, even though she was walking to her death. When her gaze met his, there was no resignation there, just dogged determination. She would go down fighting.

Suddenly, her eyes flitted past him and widened slightly. He didn't have to look to know what she had seen.

God had answered his prayers.

His men had arrived.

SEVENTEEN

Jessica expelled a whoosh of air that she didn't even realize she had been holding. Relief coursed through her, along with gratitude to a God she had only begun to know.

Two men approached from the right, weapons drawn. One was Alan. The other she didn't recognize. She glanced to the left in time to see a third round the corner of the building. Spike hadn't seen them yet. What would he do when he did? Her mind ticked through several possibilities, then settled on the most likely scenario.

He would use her as a shield while he escaped, then keep her as a hostage. Knowing Spike, once he was finished with her, he'd shoot her anyway. If he got caught, he was going to be charged with Prissy's murder. What was one more?

"Freeze!"

At the sharp command, adrenaline spiked through her and she whirled to see Spike's head swivel to the right and back again. He lunged toward her at the same moment she executed a perfect crescent kick, sending the gun sliding across the concrete air strip. A second kick to the gut knocked him down.

Shane rushed forward to keep him there, which was good, because she suddenly felt dizzy and off balance. The pain in her head had returned with a vengeance, accompanied by a ringing in both ears. Shadows began to close in from the periphery of her vision, and she sank to her knees.

Alan reached her first. He knelt down in front of her and grasped the corner of the duct tape. "This is going to hurt."

She gave him the go-ahead with a nod. When he ripped the tape from her face, his grimace was worse than her own.

"Sorry."

She sank back on her heels. "Don't worry about it. Go get Branch and Hammy. They're inside."

Alan smiled down at her. "We know. Tommy and two other FBI agents are taking them down as we speak." He stood to remove the tape from Shane's face before returning to work on freeing her hands. The other two men were almost finished restraining Spike.

She pushed herself to her feet and cupped Shane's face in her hands. "I'm so sorry. I should have listened to you. I almost got you killed."

He shook off the severed ropes and stepped forward to wrap her in a gentle embrace. "I'm all right.

We're both all right, and that's all that matters. I was praying so hard."

"So was I."

He raised his brows but didn't comment.

"Both of our prayers were answered." Or maybe it was just Shane's. But somehow, she felt hers had been heard, too. "I think I'm ready to meet this God of yours."

A brilliant smile spread across his face and lit his eyes. "That can be arranged. He's always home." He pulled her more tightly against him.

"It's finally over." She rested her head against his chest and released a satisfied sigh, sinking into the safety of his embrace. And for once in her life, she felt loved, cherished and protected. It wouldn't last. She knew that. But for a few brief moments, she would pretend. She would allow herself the luxury. Just for tonight.

Suddenly she inhaled sharply and pushed herself away.

His arms fell to his sides. "What?"

"The figurines. Hammy and Spike are hiding drugs inside the figurines."

His eyes widened. "Are you sure?"

"I'm positive. A plane just picked up a bunch of boxes. I counted twenty. Before giving Spike the money, the guy opened one of the boxes, took out a figurine and smashed it. Inside was a plastic bag filled with white powder."

A smile stretched across Shane's face, warming her from the inside out.

"You did good."

"That leather satchel you saw inside holds Spike and Hammy's payment. As you know, Branch's cut is in his pockets."

Shane nodded. "My guys will find that when they search him."

"Hopefully there are more boxes of those figurines." It would be awful if they prepared only what was sold and there was no evidence left behind.

"I *know* there are more boxes of those figurines."

"How?"

"There's a room they keep locked. I've never gotten in, but I've looked in the window, and a couple of nights ago, it was full of boxes. Now half of them are missing."

"The missing boxes went on that plane." Those left behind were likely more of the same. Plenty of evidence to convict the Driggers brothers.

She smiled with a sense of satisfaction that was bittersweet. Prissy's killers would be brought to justice. But now that Shane's drug case was wrapped up, he would be on his way, off to his next assignment.

Tommy stepped around the back of the building and approached them.

"Did you get Branch?" she asked.

"Oh, yeah. He's vigorously proclaiming his innocence, insisting he was getting ready to bring

Hammy and Spike in himself. But he's having a hard time explaining the four wads of hundreds they pulled out of his pockets."

Jessica laughed, feeling as if she had just been vindicated for years of abuse. "And what about Hammy?"

Tommy grinned. "He's jabbering away like an auctioneer on steroids. Maybe blood is thicker than water, but in Hammy's case, self-preservation is thicker than blood. He was throwing Spike under the bus before they could even get the handcuffs on him. Then he gave us the scoop on Branch and a Nick Lombardi who sets up the deals and basically acts as a thug for the Driggers boys." He looked her up and down. "And how about you? Are you okay?"

Before she could answer, Shane stepped over and wrapped a protective arm around her. "She will be. I'm going to see to it."

She swiveled her head to look at him and cocked a brow. "Oh? That's going to be a little difficult when you're off to who knows where on your next assignment."

"I don't think there's going to be a next assignment. Now that this one's over, I'm ready to give up police work and settle down."

Tommy gave Shane a mock salute and walked over to where Spike was being processed.

Jessica turned back to Shane. "You don't have to give up police work to settle down. I know of a chief of police position that just came open. And now that two brothers will be going to jail for a long time, the town is relatively safe and quiet."

"What about Tommy? He might have his eye on the chief position."

"Then he'd move up and there would still be a position open."

Shane nodded. "I could go for that. I'm not a sit-in-the-office, push-a-pen kind of guy anyway."

She smiled up at him. "So what happened to 'I never stay in one place for long'?"

"My wandering days are over. I've fallen in love with Harmony Grove and decided I might want to put down roots here." He pulled her into his arms and smiled down at her. "That is, if one spunky little pixie decides to stay, too."

"I might consider it." Her tone was amazingly smooth and nonchalant considering her stomach was doing flips. "Depends on what kind of incentive I have."

"How about a former FBI agent who's wild about you? Is that incentive enough?" He held her away from him just enough to be able to look into her eyes, his own suddenly serious. "You said that you thought I was angry with God. Well, you got me thinking. I wasn't angry with God, but I hadn't allowed Him to heal my heart, either. It was easier to vow to never love again than to risk that kind of hurt."

She reached up to cup his cheek, and he turned enough to plant a soft kiss in her palm.

"Somehow in these last few weeks, you've gotten past the walls I put up, and I'm afraid I haven't only fallen in love with Harmony Grove. I've fallen in love with its notorious former bad girl. I admire your spunk, your refusal to feel sorry for yourself, no matter what life throws your way. Your tenderness and compassion in caring for Prissy's dog, even though the last thing you wanted was the responsibility of a pet. It's everything about you, Jess. You've somehow managed to slip right past all my defenses and convince me to once again take a chance on love."

He took both of her hands in his. "I know when you came back, it was supposed to be temporary. But now that you're home, I'd like you to stay."

Home. Somehow when Shane said the word, it had a different ring. Home had always been a sad and lonely place, filled with conflict and lacking in warmth. A place she couldn't wait to escape.

But on Shane's lips, the word conjured up images of love and comfort and security. A place she longed to be.

He squeezed her hands. "I love you, Jess. I think I've loved you from the first moment I laid eyes on you." He gave a little grimace, then grinned. "Well, maybe not the *first* moment."

She smiled, too, at the image that sprang to mind—

him lying on her living room floor amidst splintered wood and shattered glass.

"But after these last few weeks, I can't imagine living my life without you." He dropped to one knee, still holding her hands.

And she held tightly to him, her whole world spinning. It was more than the blow to the head. All her senses were on overload. Shane was staying. He was giving up his career with the FBI to be with her. And he just told her he was in love with her.

Now he was kneeling…as if he was getting ready to propose. Her heart pounded in her chest, and she suddenly found it hard to breathe. She was scared to death that he was going to ask her to marry him, but equally afraid she would wake up and find it was all a dream.

Shane squeezed her hands. "What I'm trying to say is, I want to marry you. If you need some time to think about it, I understand. I just want you to know I'm not leaving. I'll be here for you…for the rest of your life, if you'll let me."

Love swelled in her chest. He understood her past and was willing to wait until she was ready. How could she say no?

She eased onto her knees in front of him. "Yes, I would love to marry you."

He released her hands to wrap her in his arms and covered her mouth with his own. Warmth filled her, along with peace, security, happiness and love—everything she had longed for all her life—and she silently thanked God for bringing her back to Harmony Grove.

She was finally home.

Anywhere with Shane would always be home.

* * * * *

Dear Reader,

For all of you who read *Midnight Shadows* and asked for another Harmony Grove novel, this is it!

I hope you enjoyed reading *Motive for Murder*. Jessica and Shane were fun characters for me to write. Jessica was tough—feisty enough to take on whatever threatened, whether a midnight intruder or her sister's killers. Three fathers who didn't love her and a string of selfish boyfriends had taught her to depend on no one except herself. Shane had suffered a tragedy that shattered his world, but not his faith. His relationship with God gave his life meaning and made him different from the other men Jess had known, which eventually led her to drop her defenses and trust not only Shane, but the God she had rejected all her life.

Many of us have faced tragedies, and during those times of extreme heartache, it is sometimes hard to go on. But Psalm 147:3 says, "God heals the brokenhearted and binds up their wounds." My prayer is that when hard times come, you will find the peace and solace that only God can offer.

Thank you for reading *Motive for Murder*. The third and final Harmony Grove novel, featuring Lexi and Alan, is coming soon. For more information about me and my books, you can check out my website at caroljpost.com. And feel free to drop me a line at caroljpost@gmail.com. I love to connect with readers!

Carol J. Post

Questions for Discussion

1. Jessica is strong, tough and self-sufficient. Could you relate to her? Why or why not?

2. Shane comes across as confident and carefree, but his smooth manner hides a lot of hurt. Did you find him to be a likable character? Why or why not?

3. Jessica's relationship with her sister is poor right from the start. Do you have any siblings? What is your relationship like? What are some issues that can cause rifts between family members? What are some ways to mend those bridges?

4. Jessica has a lot of adversity in her life and has trouble seeing God as a loving Heavenly Father. What are some good ways to respond to someone like that?

5. Shane, on the other hand, has the opposite reaction to the trauma in his life and has depended on God to give him the strength to endure. What about you? Does adversity tend to make you question the goodness of God, or does it draw you closer to Him?

6. Although Jessica holds animosity toward her sister, when she learns about the abuse Priscilla endured after she left, she is racked with guilt. This guilt makes her more determined than ever to bring her sister's killers to justice. Can you think of a time in your life or the life of someone you know when feelings of regret spurred action?

7. Shane's job as an FBI agent often requires that he lie about who he is and what he does. Do you see that as being problematic for a Christian? When, if ever, is it okay to lie? Do you believe there is such a thing as a "little white lie"?

8. Jessica has problems trusting, and as a result, keeps people at arm's length. What are some disadvantages to living this "solo" lifestyle? How can we encourage openness, both in ourselves and those we know, and establish meaningful connections?

9. Shane has convinced himself that his reason for avoiding relationships is to keep from putting another person in danger, when in actuality, his unwillingness to risk being hurt plays as big of a role in the choices he makes. Have you ever tried to convince yourself of something that wasn't true, or was only half-true?

How did that turn out? Who or what forced you to face the truth?

10. One of the complaints Jessica has with God is that He sometimes allows bad things to happen to good people. Do you or does anyone you know feel this way? How can you respond when someone questions how a loving God can allow so much evil?

11. Shane isn't angry with God over the death of his wife. But it is only after Jessica points it out that he realizes he hadn't given that hurt to God and allowed Him to heal his wounded heart. What are some ways that God uses to show us areas of our lives that we need to change?

12. Almost from the beginning, Jessica is intrigued by Shane. In what ways is he different from the other men she had known?

13. Although Shane travels a lot, he tries to attend a local church whenever he can. How important do you think a church community is in helping us heal and grow?

14. Jessica has no interest in having a pet, especially one she considers "needy." When she gets stuck with her sister's dog, she goes from planning to take him to a shelter, to consider-

ing keeping him for Priscilla's sake, to falling in love with him. Have you ever taken in a pet you didn't really want, only to have it totally win you over?

15. Were you surprised to learn the identity of the murderer? At what point did you know?

LARGER-PRINT BOOKS!

GET 2 FREE LARGER-PRINT NOVELS PLUS 2 FREE MYSTERY GIFTS

Love Inspired® SUSPENSE

RIVETING INSPIRATIONAL ROMANCE

Larger-print novels are now available...

LARGER-PRINT BOOKS!

GET 2 FREE
LARGER-PRINT NOVELS
PLUS 2 FREE
MYSTERY GIFTS

Love Inspired

Larger-print novels are now available...

Reader Service.com

Manage your account online!

- Review your order history
- Manage your payments
- Update your address

---

*We've designed
the Harlequin® Reader Service
website just for you.*

Enjoy all the features!

- Reader excerpts from any series
- Respond to mailings and special monthly offers
- Discover new series available to you
- Browse the Bonus Bucks catalog
- Share your feedback

Visit us at:
ReaderService.com